CHRISTOPHER BUSH
THE CASE OF THE PRODIGAL DAUGHTER

CHRISTOPHER BUSH was born Charlie Christmas Bush in Norfolk in 1885. His father was a farm labourer and his mother a milliner. In the early years of his childhood he lived with his aunt and uncle in London before returning to Norfolk aged seven, later winning a scholarship to Thetford Grammar School.

As an adult, Bush worked as a schoolmaster for 27 years, pausing only to fight in World War One, until retiring aged 46 in 1931 to be a full-time novelist. His first novel featuring the eccentric Ludovic Travers was published in 1926, and was followed by 62 additional Travers mysteries. These are all to be republished by Dean Street Press.

Christopher Bush fought again in World War Two, and was elected a member of the prestigious Detection Club.

He died in 1973.

CHRISTOPHER BUSH

THE CASE OF THE PRODIGAL DAUGHTER

With an introduction
by Curtis Evans

DEAN STREET PRESS

INTRODUCTION

> *Rosalind.* If it be true that good wine needs no bush [i.e., advertising], 'tis true that a good play needs no epilogue. Yet to good wine, they do use good bushes, and good plays prove the better by the help of good epilogues.
>
>   –SHAKESPEARE, Epilogue, *As You Like It*

THE decade of the 1960s saw the sun finally begin to set on that storied generation which between the First and Second World Wars gave us detective fiction's Golden Age. Taking account of both deaths and retirements, by the late Sixties only a bare half-dozen pre-World War Two members of the Detection Club were still plying their deliciously deceptive craft: Agatha Christie, Anthony Gilbert (Lucy Beatrice Malleson), Gladys Mitchell, John Dickson Carr, Nicholas Blake and Christopher Bush, the subject of this introduction. Bush himself would pass away, at the age of eighty-seven, in 1973, having published, at the age of eighty-two, his sixty-third Ludovic Travers detective novel, *The Case of the Prodigal Daughter*, in the United Kingdom in the spring of 1968.

In the United States Bush's final detective novel did not appear until late November 1969, about four months after the horrific Manson murders in the tarnished Golden State of California. Implicating the triple terrors of sex, drugs and rock and roll (not to mention almost inconceivably bestial violence), the Manson slayings could not have strayed farther from the whimsically escapist "death as a game" aesthetic of Golden Age of detective fiction. Increasingly in the decade capable of producing psychedelic psychopaths like Charles Manson and his "family," the few remaining survivors of the Golden Age of detective fiction increasingly deemed themselves men and women far out of time. In his detective fiction John Dickson Carr, an incurable romantic, prudently beat a retreat from the present into the pleasanter pages of the past, setting his tales in bygone historical eras where he felt vastly more at home. With varying success Agatha Christie made a brave effort to stay abreast of the times (*Third Girl, Endless Night*), but ultimately her strivings to understand what was going on around her collapsed into the utter incoherence of *Passenger to Frankfurt* and *Postern of Fate*, by general consensus the worst mystery novels that Dame Agatha ever put down on paper.

In his detective fiction Christopher Bush, who was not quite two years older than Christie, managed rather better than the Queen of Crime to keep up with all the unsettling goings-on around him, while never forswearing the Golden Age article of faith that the primary purpose of a crime writer is pleasingly to puzzle his/her readers. And, in contrast with Christie and Carr, Bush knew when it was time to lay down his pen (or turn off his dictation machine, as the case may be), thereby allowing him to make his exit from the stage on a comparatively high note. Indeed, Christopher Bush's concluding baker's dozen of detective novels, which he published between 1957 and 1968 (and which have now been reprinted, after more than a half-century, by Dean Street Press), makes a generally fine epilogue, or coda, to the author's impressive corpus of crime fiction, which first began to see the light of day way back in the jubilant Jazz Age. These are, readers will find, "good bushes" (to punningly borrow from Shakespeare), providing them with ample intelligent detective entertainment as Bush's longtime series sleuth Ludovic Travers, in the luminous twilight of his career, makes his final forays into ingenious criminal investigation.

*

In the last thirteen Ludovic Travers mystery novels, Travers' *entrée* to his cases continues to come through his ownership of the Broad Street Detective Agency. Besides Travers we also regularly encounter his elegant wife, Bernice (although sometimes his independent-minded spouse is away on excursions of her own), his proverbially loyal secretary, Bertha Munney, his top Broad Street op, Hallows (another one named French, presumably inspired by Bush's late Detection Club colleague Freeman Wills Crofts, pops up occasionally), John Hill of the United Assurance Agency, who brings Travers many of his cases, and Scotland Yard's Inspector Jewle and Sergeant Matthews, who after the first of these final novels, *The Case of the Treble Twist* (in the U. S. *Triple Twist*), are promoted, respectively, to Superintendent and Inspector. (The Yard's ex-Superintendent George Wharton, now firmly retired from any form of investigative work whatsoever, is mentioned just once by Ludo, when, in *The Case of the Dead Man Gone*, he passingly imparts that he and Wharton recently had lunch together.)

For all practical purposes Travers, who during the Golden Age was a classic gentleman amateur snooper like Philo Vance and Lord Peter Wimsey, now functions fully as a professional private eye—although one, to be sure, who is rather posher than the rest. While some reviewers referred to Travers as England's Philip Marlowe, in fact he little resembles the general run of love and leave 'em/hate and beat 'em brand of brutish American P. I.'s, favoring a nice cup of coffee (a post-war change from tea), a good pipe and the occasional spot of sherry to the frequent snatches of liquor and cigarettes favored by most of his American brethren and remaining faithful to his spouse despite encountering a succession of sexy women, not all of them, shall we say, virtuously inclined.

This was a formula which throughout the period maintained a devoted audience on both sides of the Atlantic consisting, one surmises, of readers (including crime writers Anthony Berkeley, Nicholas Blake and the late Alan Hunter, creator of Inspector George Gently) who preferred their detectives something less than hard-boiled. Travers himself sneers at the hugely popular (and psychotically violent) postwar American private eye Mike Hammer, commenting of an American couple in *The Case of the Treble Twist*: "She was a woman of considerable culture; his ran about as far as Mickey Spillane" [a withering reference to Mike Hammer's creator]. Yet despite his manifest disdain for Mike Hammer, an ugly American if ever there were one, Christopher Bush and his wife Florence in the spring of 1957 had traveled to New York aboard the RMS *Queen Elizabeth*, and references by him to both the United States and Canada became more frequent in the books which followed this trip.

Certainly *The Case of the Treble Twist* (1957) features tough customers and an exceptionally cruel murder, yet it is also one of Bush's most ingeniously contrived cases from the Fifties, full of charm, treacherous deception and, yes, plenty of twists, including one that is a real sockaroo (to borrow, as Bush occasionally did, from

American idiom). Similarly clever is *The Case of the Running Man* (1958), which draws, as several earlier Bush books had, on the author's profound love and knowledge of antiques. By this time Bush and his wife, their coffers having burgeoned from the proceeds of his successful mysteries, resided in the quaint medieval market town of Lavenham, Suffolk at the Great House, a splendidly decorated fourteenth-century structure with an elegant Georgian-era façade which he and Florence purchased in 1953 and resided in until their deaths. The dashing author, whom in 1967 *Chicago Tribune* mystery reviewer Alice Crombie swooningly dubbed "one of the handsomest mystery writers on either side of the Channel or Atlantic," also drove a Jaguar, beloved by James Bond films of late, well into his eighties.

The Case of the Running Man includes that Golden Age detective fiction staple, a family tree, but more originally the novel features as a major character a black American man, Sam, the devoted chauffeur of the wealthy murder victim. Sam, who reminds Ludovic Travers of Rochester, "Jack Benny's factotum of television and radio," is an interesting and sincerely treated individual, although as Anthony Boucher amusingly pronounced at the time in the *New York Times Book Review*, he speaks "a dialect never heard by mortal ear"—an odd compounding of "American Negro" and London cockney.

The Case of the Careless Thief (1959) takes Ludo to Sandbeach, "the Blackpool of the South Coast," as the American jacket blurb puts it, with "a dozen hotels, a race track, a dog track, a music hall and two enormous dance halls." Anthony Boucher deemed this hard-hitting, tricky tale, which draws to strong effect on contemporary events in England, "one of Ludovic Travers' best cases." Likewise hard-hitting are *The Case of the Sapphire Brooch* (1960) and *The Case of the Extra Grave* (1961), complex tales of murderous mésalliances with memorably grim conclusions. The plot of *The Case of the Dead Man Gone* (1961) topically involves refugee relief groups, while *The Case of the Heavenly Twin* (1963) opens with a case of a creative criminal couple forging American Express Travelers Checks, concerning which Americans of a certain age will recall actor Karl Malden sternly enjoining, in a long-running television advertising campaign: "Don't leave home without them." In contrast with many of his crime writing contemporaries (judging from the tone of their work), Bush actually learned to watch and enjoy television, although in *The Case of Three-Ring Puzzle*, a tale of violently escalating intrigue, Travers dryly references Scottish philosopher Thomas Carlyle's famous observation that England's population consisted of "mostly fools" when he comments: "I guess he wasn't too far out at that. But rather remarkable an estimate perhaps, considering that in his day there were no television commercials."

Of Bush's final five Ludovic Travers detective novels, published between 1964 and 1968, when the Western World, in the eyes of many, was going from whimsically mod to utterly mad, the best are, in my estimation, the cases of *The Jumbo Sandwich* (1965), *The Good Employer* (1966) and *The Prodigal Daughter* (1968). In *Sandwich* a crisp case of a defrauded (and jilted) gentry lady friend of Ludo's metamorphoses into a smorgasbord of, as the American book jacket puts it, "blackmail, black magic, a black sheep, and murder." It all culminates in a confrontation on a lonely Riviera beach in France, setting of some of Ludovic Travers' earliest cases, between Ludo and a desperate killer, in which Bernice plays an unexpectedly active part. Ludo again travels to France in the highly classic *Employer*, which draws most engagingly on the sleuth's (and the author's) dabbling in the world of art and is dedicated to his distinguished Lavenham artist friends, the couple Reginald and Rosalie Brill, who resided next door to Bush and his wife at the fourteenth-century Little Hall, then an art student hostel for which the Brills served as guardians. In *The Guardian* Francis Iles (aka Golden Age crime writer Anthony Berkeley) pronounced that *Employer* represented Bush "at his most ingenious."

Finally, in *Daughter* Travers finds himself tasked with recovering the absconded teenage offspring of domineering Dora Marport, sober-sided head of the organization Home and Family, which is righteously devoted to "the fostering, so to speak, of family life as the stoutest bulwark against the encroachment of ever-more numerous hostile forces: sex and violence in literature, films and on television; pornography generally, and the erosion of responsibility and the capability for sacrifice by the welfare state." Can Travers, a Great War veteran who made his debut in detective fiction in 1926, bridge the generation gap in late-Sixties London? Ludo may prefer Bach to the Beatles, but in this, the last of his recorded cases, he proves more "with it" than one might have expected. All in All, *Daughter* makes a rewarding finish to one of the longest-running and most noteworthy sleuth series in British detective fiction.

Curtis Evans

PART I
HOME AND FAMILY

CHAPTER 1
THE ROBBERY

IT WAS a wet, raw October morning. You remember what a poor summer and a dreary autumn we had—here and there a little sunshine but mostly rain and high winds. I had stayed on a few moments in bed that morning after waking, and the wind was still howling round the flats and the rain dashing against the lounge windows.

It was snug enough in my office at the Broad Street Detective Agency. Bertha had laid out the correspondence as usual and I was just running a preliminary eye over it when the buzzer went from her room. Mr. Hicks of United Assurance was on the line.

United Assurance is easily our most valuable client, and when anyone rings from there, I push everything aside and get ready to listen.

"That you, Mr. Travers?"

"It is," I said. "Haven't seen you for quite a time. How are you?"

"Hot and bothered," he said. "Are you too busy to spare us an hour or so straight away?"

"At Lombard Street?"

"No," he said, "At Stepney. You know it at all?"

I said I could find my way around.

"Well, it's a cul-de-sac just off Witlow Street. Childers Way, a few yards on from a pub called the Greyhound. A firm of wholesale chemists—Garrod and Bland. Oh, and is Bob Hallows available too?"

I said he was.

"A fire, is it?"

"No, no. Just something else in which we're interested. Be seeing you then."

As I may have told you before, there are four of us at Broad Street. Norris looks after accounts and allocates jobs for various operatives. Hallows specialises in cases of suspected arson but is just as good at everything else. Between cases for private clients I fill in with anything. Lastly there's Bertha Munney, who's secretary-receptionist. Like Bob Hallows, she's been with the firm since its beginning, which was nearly thirty years ago.

In common with most firms in our line of business, we have our rush of jobs. This was one of our quieter periods, which was why Hallows was at Broad Street. Stepney's no great distance away, and a quarter of an hour after Hicks had called me, we were in Childers Way. It was a mournful-looking neighbourhood and the misty rain didn't make it any better. The cul-de-sac street itself was about a hundred yards long. It was fairly wide, with what looked like warehouses on each side, together with a few parked cars. Till you neared the far wall, that is. That end wall was a good twelve feet high, its rounded top thick with broken glass. Beyond it was the railway.

Nicely short of the wall to the right were the premises of Garrod and Bland. In the dinginess of that cul-de-sac they stood out like a tailor's model in a collection of scare-crows: two storeys of metal and plate glass, clean as a new pin. Even the tall doors that seemed to lead back to the loading and unloading departments looked as if they'd been just erected. A few yards farther on was the main entrance. The door opened as if it had been oiled.

Hicks was waiting for us just inside. He's just over six feet—slightly shorter than myself—with thinnish blond hair and a blond moustache which somehow makes him look as if he ought to be wearing pince-nez. His manner's just a bit on the abrupt side, but we've always got along well together.

With him was a thickly built, much shorter man of about his own age—forty—whom he introduced as Fred Palmer, one of his inspectors. He said it would save time if Hallows and Palmer got busy straightaway, with Palmer explaining as they went along. He was to tell me all about it while we stood there in the empty entrance hall.

Garrod and Bland were wholesale chemists: distributors, if you like, to the east of London for two of the big manufacturing companies. They carried a very large stock made up of a multiplicity of items. The premises were only two years old, which accounted for the newness of their looks; and United Assurance had been involved from the moment they came to Stepney from their former premises in Tottenham which had been partially destroyed by fire.

"We had to regard this place as vulnerable," Hicks said. "I should say specially vulnerable, so there were certain things we had to insist on before we were prepared to insure. The place is fairly isolated, as you've seen for yourself, and all wholesale chemists are more open to robbery than they were, say, ten years ago. The traffic in drugs, for instance, and the whole range of stimulant pills—"

"Like Purple Hearts?"

"Exactly. But, as I was saying, the firm recognised the vulnerability and were prepared to co-operate in every way. Palmer, whom you've just seen, was chiefly responsible for the installation of the security system and, as soon as he gave his okay, we talked terms. The place has been absolutely safe ever since. Till last night."

"A burglary?"

"Yes. With violence. Fairlow, the night-watchman, was struck on the head and is now in hospital on the danger list. He was an utterly reliable man: able to deal with any ordinary crises: a big, strong fellow with all his wits about him. The attack must have taken place between ten and midnight. Part of the security system was for him to report at ten to the local police-station. He reported every two hours and, when he didn't report at midnight, they came to find out why."

"And you're checking up now on the rest of the security system?"

"That's right. The police have only just left. They were here half the night and found nothing. Never a fingerprint or a sign of entry. Their idea is that whoever did the job must have managed somehow to conceal himself on the premises during the day."

There'd been a slight droop of the lip.

"And you don't believe it."

"I don't. I don't think there's anywhere he could have hidden and I don't think he could have negotiated the system of alarms."

"Then how *did* he—or could it be they?—get in?"

"That's why we'd like your views," he said. "Hallows is checking security with Palmer and we may know more when they've finished. We might do worse now than go to the office." As soon as we were out of that small entrance hall, we heard plenty of sounds of life. Business was going on as usual behind the scenes. In the manager's office was the general manager himself, a man of about thirty-five named Yoxton. With him was the managing director: a much older man—Vernon Bland. Hicks introduced me and asked how things were going.

"Think we've just about finished," Bland said. "It's been rather difficult. Not an easy check-up. Very involved. Wouldn't you people like some coffee while we go into it?"

He rang through while Yoxton saw us seated.

"What you may be surprised at is the smallness of the actual bulk involved," he told us. "We reckon the whole amount could have been taken away in a couple of medium-sized suitcases."

"Like a pocketful of diamonds?"

"In a way, yes. High value in small bulk."

A trim secretary brought in the coffee. We settled down again.

"Talking of bulk," Bland said. "We've got to remember that the cost of the stock as carried by us bears little relation to the illicit disposal cost, especially if the disposal is at first-hand. Multiply by ten and you still may not have reached the total. This is what we now know to be the complete list of the missing drugs."

It was pretty formidable, even if there was little that I actually understood. Heroin and cocaine, yes.

"These pills under the amphetamine range," I said. "Are they what's commonly known as Purple Hearts?"

"In a way, yes," Yoxton said. "Benzedrine, dexedrine, methedrine, preludin, and so on. They're the ones that lead to horrors. Among the elite—even teenagers—they're known as bennies, dexies, blueys and so on. Popular names of certain varieties are Purple Hearts, Black Bombers, Black and White Minstrels."

Once inside that building, the entrants had had an easy time as we saw when we walked round. Everywhere was the antiseptic smell of a hospital, with the rows of stock cupboards and shelving clean as if just scrubbed, and meticulously docketed. Containers came all shapes and sizes and all one had to do was remove from a shelf and drop into a bag.

"No need to ask if the police found any finger-prints?" I said.

As far as Bland knew, they'd found nothing: never a print or a trace of entry. I asked where the unconscious Fairlow was actually found. It was in a widish passage that led from the entrance hall past the private stairs to the first floor and on to the stock rooms. Set in the floor hard against the wall just beyond where Fairlow had been lying was what looked like a rubber door-stop. Yoxton told me it was an alarm. All one had to do was put a foot on it.

"Unexpected things in unexpected places," Hicks said. "Wherever you are in the building you can raise an alarm in practically a second. Or an intruder might raise one for himself."

Palmer and Hallows joined us as we were standing there. Everything they'd seen had been in perfect shape. How an entry could have been made was beyond credibility.

"The age of miracles is over," Bland said. "The fact remains that an entry *was* made. And it wasn't done with mirrors."

"About Fairlow himself," Hallows said. "You're dead sure about his reliability?"

Yoxton was a bit terse. "No question. The fact that he was badly hurt answers that."

Something was beginning to puzzle me when things were seen from an unbiased angle. I asked Bland if I was right in thinking Fairlow's night quarters were on the first floor.

"Quite right," he told me. "You'd like to see them?"

"No," I said. "What I would like to know is what he was doing down here at all. Presumably it was after ten and he'd made his all clear report, so why did he come down again?"

"Maybe he heard something."

"Then it must have been from outside," I said. "We've got to take the evidence of our senses that no entry could possibly have been made. So let's assume that he heard a noise. The position of the body with its head towards the stairs shows he was coming back from somewhere and that somewhere could have been only the entrance hall. Since nobody could have hidden, the assailant who struck him from behind must have been admitted in good faith through the main door and been accompanying him to his room."

"Incredible!" Yoxton said. "Besides, where the body was actually found isn't proof of where he was knocked out. Also he was bound and gagged and that might have meant moving him."

"I think Mr. Travers is working on the right lines," Hallows told him. "It explains the inexplicable. I'm beginning to be sure Fairlow let someone in through the main door. Therefore it was someone he either knew and trusted or who convinced him he had the right to enter. That may mean a thorough checking of all your staff."

The argument was getting a bit heated by the time we were back in the head office. Bland was about to leave in any case. The police had called him not long after midnight and he was going home for a clean-up and a meal. Before he left he wanted the latest on Fairlow from the hospital. As he said, Fairlow had to have only a moment or two of consciousness and we'd have the answers.

A minute or two and he was on the line. You could tell from his face that things were none too good. He was shaking his head as he replaced the receiver.

"There was something like consciousness about an hour ago," he told us. "The officer by his bed just managed to catch a sort of whisper that sounded like, 'Police,' and that was all. He's now in an extremely critical condition."

"*Police*," Hallows said. "I don't want to rush too far ahead, but mightn't we have the answer?"

The main door bell went and Hallows went down to investigate. What he saw was a couple of uniformed police.

"Remember all the lorries that are held up by what appear to be police?"

"You're right," Nicks said. "It's the perfect explanation." I wanted to know if the police knew what had caused the blow. No one knew, not that it mattered too much. The usual blunt instrument would fit the case. I said we might even carry things a bit further from just the admission of the fake police.

"As I see it, the blow was a particularly heavy and vicious one. Only the most callous of criminals would hit to kill, so I think there must have been some sort of emergency. Possibly Fairlow had begun to suspect something. Perhaps he quickened his step as he approached that floor signal or made some other false move."

Another five minutes and we were ready to disperse and, on the whole, we were a reasonably satisfied assortment. Palmer must have been delighted. The theory showed that there'd been no flaw in the system for which he'd been responsible. Bland knew there'd be no arguments about insurance and Nicks could make a highly satisfactory report. Hallows and I had no grumbles. We'd at least given value for our fee.

We did one last thing, and by arrangement with Bland. The local police headquarters was only three minutes away, so we dropped in to see if anything we could report would be of help. The inspector in charge of the case was at the Yard but we saw his sergeant. Once he'd got over his lack of faith in private detective agencies, he began to co-operate and when we left we'd made quite a statement.

Just before four o'clock that afternoon Bertha had brought in our usual tea and Mallows and I were still mulling over that case when who should ring but our old friend Superintendent Jewle. A few pleasantries and he came to the point.

"By the way, I'm told you were at Stepney this morning."

It was a typical gambit. It threw the ball straight away into our court. Not that there was anything devious about it: just Jewle's special routine. As I've said, he's a friend: you might say—outside business—a close friend. Hallows and I and Jewle have been like that for years. Professionally we keep on a straight line. If there's ever a slight deviation, well, you can't always help a skid. If he acquires information that might help a case of ours, he passes it on. We do the same.

I told him why we'd been there. He knows all about our relationships with United Assurance in any event. I added that as far as we were concerned, we were extremely unlikely to have anything further to do with the case. Everything was in the hands of the police.

"Exactly," he said. "But about that report you and Bob made at Stepney. You still honestly believe it fool-proof?"

"No," I said. "What I think is that it's a logical explanation of what had once seemed incomprehensible circumstances. But tell me something. What's a High-Up like yourself doing with an ordinary burglary?"

"It isn't," he said quietly. "Fairlow died half-an-hour ago. We're dealing with a matter of murder."

Hallows, listening on the other phone, gave a sudden shake of the head. Whether it was a sign of grief or because there was something he didn't want me to say, I didn't know. At any rate, I cut things short as tactfully as I could.

"Terrible," I said. "He seems to have been a really good man. Anything else we can do to help, you can rely on us to do."

"I know that," he said. "You may have helped quite a lot already. By the way, if it's any interest, the blow was almost certainly struck with the butt of a hefty gun."

It was one of those happenings where you'd give a good deal to help but know that you've no earthly chance of doing so. In any case, what could we have done? Jewle said something of the sort when we had lunch together— at his request, by the way—a few days later. Already he was at a dead end.

"All we have is that it bears a close resemblance to a case about six months ago," he told me. "There the manager of a chemist's shop that was just closing for the night was manhandled by a couple of fake police: one uniformed and the other supposed to be an inspector, warrant card and all. My idea is that it was a kind of try-out by the same couple. The Stepney job was a move up to higher things, so to speak."

"But the information. How was that acquired?"

"Well," he said, "they'd get various wholesale chemists from the telephone directory, then they'd inspect and choose. Next they'd watch the staff and maybe have a sort of general chat in his pub with an employee. Done skilfully, that would give them the security arrangements. Not that it's going to help us. No employee's going to admit that he gave the firm's secrets away, even inadvertently. Our only hope is to get a whisper from somewhere."

"Frustrating," I said.

"It's maddening. When I think of my own kids, I wonder whose kids are going to be on the buying end when all that dope gets peddled. And the peddling bastards lining their greedy pockets. It makes my blood boil. Not only that. It mayn't be long before they'll be planning another job."

I asked if the proposed registration of clubs was going to be any help. Mightn't it lead to more open, and therefore more risky, pushing? He said it would touch only the fringe. Every resort of teenagers was a potential pushers' paradise. Word soon got around and those out for kicks wouldn't have far to go.

That was the last I was to hear for a long time of the Stepney affair. A day or two after that meeting with Jewle

I was to get busy over a private matter for the Agency. That was towards the end of October.

CHAPTER 2
HOME AND FAMILY

IT WAS just after ten o'clock. Hallows was away for a couple of days on a job in Newcastle and I was helping Norris with accounts when Bertha buzzed through to say that a Lady Marport was on the line. I think I raised my eyebrows as I picked up the receiver.

"The Broad Street Detective Agency. Travers speaking."

"Ah, Mr. Travers. This is Dora Marport. I've just spoken to your secretary and she assured me you were in."

"Indeed, yes," I said. "What can we do for you, Lady Marport?"

"I'd like you to come and see me. At once if possible."

"Where?"

"At our headquarters. Eighteen Kelvin Road, St. John's Wood."

"Pardon me," I said, and made the tone as deprecatory as I could, "but you mentioned headquarters."

"Of course! The headquarters of Home and Family."

"Ah, yes," I said. "And you couldn't give me any idea of what you wanted to consult me about."

"It's exceedingly private," she told me tartly. "I wouldn't mention it to anybody if a friend hadn't given me your name and assured me you could be implicitly trusted."

"That was extremely obliging of them," I said, and I hope there was no touch of sarcasm. "Whether we can be of service to you or not, everything that passes between us will be highly confidential."

"Thank you," she told me graciously. "I shall expect you, then, as soon as you can come."

"That should be in about half-an-hour," I glanced up at the clock. "Allowing, of course, for the traffic."

I asked Bertha to come in. She'll never be Miss Universe, but at forty-five she has an excellent figure and the slightly snub nose gives her face what I might call a piquant look. She's intelligent and most efficient. I asked her why she was smiling.

"It was the sound of her," she said.

I had to admit that she'd sounded pretty formidable.

"This Home and Family business, Bertha. What is it exactly? Some sort of women's society?"

She shrugged her shoulders. "I don't really know. I seem to have heard of it and I think it's some sort of guild. For the preservation of family life. Something like that. But wouldn't Mrs. Travers know?"

I asked her to get Bernice for me, and luckily she was still in. The seconds were ticking away from the half-hour I'd specified.

"Bertha was right," Bernice said. "It's a society whose aim is to bring the importance of family life before the public. It's the family as the—well, the nucleus of everything that's important in national life. I can't put it any better than that. But why do you ask?"

"Just something that's turned up here," I said. "So do something for me if you can. Ask around among your friends and get me all you can on this Home and Family thing: especially the Lady Marport who seems to have quite a lot to do with it."

I added that there was no enormous hurry, though I'd like to have the information by the evening. Then I asked Bertha to go through any reference books and unearth what she could.

I was lucky in the trains. When I got out at St. John's Wood I still had a chance to make it on time. I wasn't so lucky in getting to Kelvin Road. Number 18 was late Victorian and a fairly happy attempt at late Georgian. There seemed quite a garden at the back but the front was only some twenty feet from the road. On the brick post that held the wrought-iron gate was a brass plate—

REGISTERED OFFICES OF
HOME AND FAMILY
Hours: 9.0 a.m. to 5.0 p.m.
Closed on Saturdays.

The door was open. Immediately inside, a notice protruded from the wall—

ENQUIRIES

and on the frosted glass of its door black lettering said I was to go straight in. In what was little more than a snug cubby-hole, a pretty girl was putting circulars into envelopes. She glanced up from her table and gave an enquiring smile. I had to speak up. The partition walls looked thin and just beyond them was a furious rattling of typewriters.

"My name's Travers. I have an appointment with Lady Marport."

She got up at once. I followed into the outer passage. It looked to me as if the innards of that house had been subdivided with laminated wood and plaster board to form a series of offices. We stopped at the far end. My guide tapped at the door and put a head inside.

"Mr. Travers is here, Lady Marport."

"Then tell him to come in, Helen."

Helen gave me a queer sort of look, half resigned, half mischievous. I stepped through the door into quite a large and extremely comfortable office.

"Take a seat, Mr. Travers, will you? Extremely kind of you to get here so soon. And excuse me for a minute. There's something I definitely must finish."

She was a rather floridly handsome woman in her late forties. She was quite plainly dressed in skirt and jumper but a mink coat was hanging on the stand in the far corner. Everything about her and the room itself looked unobtrusively efficient. There'd been a quick, formal smile when she'd glanced up at me but there'd been no aggression in the voice: just formal words for a formal situation. I wondered more than ever what it was she wanted to consult me about. If the unruffled manner was anything to go by, then it couldn't be of any great importance.

All at once she pushed the papers aside and got to her feet. She was very tall for a woman and she had the figure of a woman a good ten years younger. She was giving me a shrewd look as she held out her hand.

"Good-morning again, Mr. Travers. It was good of you to come. A horrible morning, isn't it. You'd like some coffee?"

I smiled and said I certainly wouldn't refuse it. From the way she disregarded that slight flippancy I guessed I'd better keep to strict formality.

A door at the far corner opened and a youngish but highly efficient-looking woman came in.

"Oh, Georgina, you might see that we have coffee. And take these, will you."

"Certainly, Lady Marport."

Georgina went out with the papers at which her chief had been working. Lady Marport settled back in the comfortable roundness of the swivel chair.

"A most excellent secretary," she told me. "A first-class secretary's a godsend, don't you agree?"

"I do," I said. "All the difference between smooth running and near chaos."

"Admirably put, if you'll pardon my saying so. You were at Cambridge, weren't you?"

I stifled the flippancy.

"Indeed yes. You have any connections yourself?"

"No," she said. "With Oxford—yes. My late husband was at Christchurch, as you may probably know."

Georgina brought in a handsome tray with all the trimmings for coffee. I said I'd have white with a little sugar and I was thinking about the woman who was pouring it, and trying to make some real contact. That voice of hers was no longer as aggressive as it had been on the telephone. It reminded me in a way of a radiogram I'd once had to send back to the makers, the clearness of its tone spoilt by a curious stridency.

"And now shall we get down to the business which I wish to consult you about," she said. "I regret to say it has to do with my own daughter. Perhaps you'd better read this."

She picked up her handbag from the carpet, found a letter and handed it to me.

Croft House

Wimbledon,

14-10-66

Dear Mother,

I'm afraid I can't reconcile myself to fitting into your scheme of things. You've refused to take me seriously but now you have to. From now on I'm determined to live my own life.

There'll be no point in trying to find out where I am, but from time to time I shall let you know how I am. I presume you'll be interested in at least that much.

I'm sorry I had to resort to a certain amount of subterfuge, but it was the only way things could be done. I think you'd better get into touch with Milden Close. I told Miss Roe you'd be writing her on your return.

Beryl.

"Croft House is your private address?"

"Yes," she said. "Perhaps I'd better explain. The family home was Lamington Court—you may have heard of it. It's in the Bicester country and my husband used to hunt regularly. After his death—it was actually in the hunting field—my mother suddenly died too. It was she who really founded Home and Family, so I decided to take over her house at Wimbledon. It was her wish, too, that I should succeed her in Home and Family, and Wimbledon was particularly handy. My secretary lives there too and she sees to my private correspondence every morning before coming on here. I usually get here at about ten o'clock."

"Perfectly clear," I said, and took out my notebook. "May I have everything else you can tell me about your daughter?"

"Well, she's fairly tall and slimly built. She has my own figure at her age and my colouring. Her seventeenth birthday was in February last."

"Schools?"

"Of course. But perhaps I'd better outline what I always had in mind for her, which was to carry on the line of succession here. She went to an excellent private school—St. Winifred's, near Oxford—and this autumn term she was going to Milden Close, which is a very fine finishing school also near Oxford. Later it was intended she should go to my own college—Somerville. You find that quite clear?"

"Perfectly. And the mention in the letter of your own return. Has that any significance?"

"Indeed it has. Every significance. Beryl should have gone to Milden Close this early September, but a few days before she was due there, I had to leave for a tour of America and Canada. We have branches there now and it was necessary to see to their organisation and possible enlargement. I actually returned last Wednesday and I found this letter."

"And the subterfuge to which she refers?"

Her lips clamped tight. What was coming was probably the Abomination in High Places.

"What she did was unpardonable. She rang Miss Roe saying she was one of my secretaries and I was supposed to have written from New York changing all the arrangements. Beryl would not be going to Milden Close after all, and on my return I'd see Miss Roe—the Principal—

personally and reimburse her for any breach of contract and so on. Miss Roe took it all as gospel." The lips clamped tight again. "It was a highly delicate situation but everything's settled now, thank heaven."

That, I said, was all very clear. Who else besides herself knew the facts?

"My secretary and my housekeeper, and my solicitors. They're in Chancery Lane—Bright, Hargreaves and Bright. Beryl has a personal allowance of three hundred a year from her grandmother's estate. If she marries—subject to my approval—or comes of age, whichever should happen first, she inherits quite a large sum of money from her father's estate."

"Has she any relations?"

"Unhappily, no. My own father died tragically and Sir George was much older than myself. His parents died some years ago. We were both only children."

"And Beryl's friends?"

"None. At least that I could possibly approve of. A year or two ago my housekeeper had to make a complaint and I had to forbid Beryl to bring such people to the house. Modern teenagers and wholly irresponsible. You see them on television. Programmes like *Top of the Pops*." She gave a little shudder. "You probably dislike them as much as I."

I said I always avoided them. To me it was like some strange tribe doing their still stranger tribal dances.

"But to get back to the enquiry. I should have to see your housekeeper. It's quite possible Beryl let fall something to her while you were away. Have you asked her about it?"

"She knew nothing. Beryl told her that plans had been changed and she wasn't going to Milden Close after all. It was on May's day off that Beryl must have removed all her things. She either hired a taxi or else one of her friends moved the things for her."

"What about the clothes that were taken? Could any of them be described?"

"Again I couldn't say. It's a hard thing for a mother to admit, but she never consulted me about anything, especially her clothes. She had her allowance and she bought whatever she thought fit, except the things obligatory for school. Ever since her father died she'd had that streak of independence. It was as if she was living behind a wall, at least as far as I was concerned. I think she wore the kind of clothes girls of her age wear nowadays. The sort of thing one buys in the King's Road."

"What about school friends? Did she have any stay with her or bring them home?"

"Not for the last two years."

"How did she spend her holidays?"

"I wanted her here, just to get an insight, and then, about a year ago, she refused to come any more. Definitely refused. She had an incredible stubbornness, Mr. Travers."

"So for the last year you haven't known what she did with herself in her holidays?"

"All I've known has been at second-hand through my housekeeper." She leaned forward as if dictating the name. "Mrs. Forster—May Forster. She's a widow. One of the old staff at Lamington Court. Her late husband was our head gardener."

"I take it I can question her—subject to the same reservations?"

I could.

"And photographs," I said. "I shall need them for identification."

She clicked her tongue in annoyance.

"Again, you'll hardly believe this but I haven't one. There were one or two at Wimbledon, but Beryl must have taken them. It was all part of that disappearance plan. Or as if she didn't want to leave anything of herself behind."

Something told me I'd about exhausted the possible sources of information, so I got down to business. I said I'd gathered that she wanted us to find her daughter.

She did, and urgently. "I just can't have this worry hanging over my head, Mr. Travers. Even by itself it would be bad enough, but in just under three weeks we have our annual conference at the Albert Hall and you know now what that must mean to me."

I drew up a couple of brief agreements. She didn't quibble about terms: in fact the pounds I quoted might have been pence. I took special pains to point out that the reference to "within a reasonable time" was in her own interests. Often there came a time in a case when it would be a waste of the client's money to continue.

"It won't come to that," she answered me. "I'm sure you'll find her."

I don't know if it was some easily summoned emotion, but I thought for a moment she was going to burst into tears.

"She's all that's left to me. She must be found. And be brought to realise the terrible thing she's done to me."

"We'll do our best," I said, and got to my feet. "But even if she's still in London, London's a very big place. But we'll do everything we can, even if it isn't going to be easy. Just one other question and one you may not like. Why haven't you been to the police?"

She looked horrified. "The police! And have it published abroad that I'm incapable of controlling my own daughter!"

"They're discreet," I said. "I could assure you there'd be no publicity."

"I think I know best," she told me just a bit tartly. "With you at least I'm sure there'll be no publicity. You have children of your own?"

"Unhappily, no."

"But you're married?"

"Indeed, yes."

Her face suddenly brightened. "Then your wife may be one of our members."

I shook a regretful head. "I hardly think she is. At least she's never mentioned it."

"But she ought to be a member." The smile was a bit arch. "Who isn't for us is against us. You must take her some of our literature."

She went back to the desk and spoke over the intercom. In less than no time Georgina was bringing in a neat bundle of brochures, pamphlets and leaflets.

"It's uncommonly kind of you," I said. "I'm sure my wife will be interested."

"She should come to the conference meeting," Georgina said.

"Indeed, yes. Let me know in good time, Mr. Travers, and I'll reserve a ticket."

A few seconds and I was walking back along Kelvin Road. At the moment I could be sure of nothing: all I had was a series of impressions, and what they added up to was this, even if it might ultimately prove to be wrong. It was that from the moment of my entering Dora Marport's office until the moment when the last scant reverberations of her voice had left my ears, I'd more and more begun to feel a wonder: not that Beryl Marport had cut the maternal apron strings but that her mother should so affrontedly find the whole thing utterly inexplicable. It was a case of the man who claims to be Napoleon. No logic or device can prove to him that he isn't, and for that most excellent of reasons that he knows he *is*.

On the journey back in the Underground I read some of that literature: reports of annual conferences, statistical reports and some pure proselytism. The Guild—which seems the best thing to call it—had a far bigger membership than I'd imagined. Its president was just inside the fringes of royalty; its treasurer a well-known life-peeress, and its list of vice-presidents was thickly sprinkled with titles.

As for its aims and objects, Bernice had admirably summed them up—the fostering, so to speak, of family life as the stoutest bulwark against the encroachment of ever-more-numerous hostile forces: sex and violence in literature, films and on television: pornography generally, and the erosion of responsibility and the capability for sacrifice by the Welfare State. There was quite a persuasive article by an ex-Cabinet Minister on the Victorian home and an indictment of its detractors. By the time I'd reached my station I had a good idea of what Home and Family was all about.

Except that it created a background, what I'd read was no help at all. My problem was not concerned with Society with either a big or little letter: it was concerned with a couple of women: one whom an almost morbid dedication to public service continued to dominate, and the other whom that same dedication had come to nauseate. Beryl Marport had had no wish to be groomed for her mother's kind of stardom. By the way, it didn't seem extravagant to regard Beryl as a woman. That had been her mother's mistake, but I couldn't let it be my own. In a few months Beryl would be eighteen, and I'd recently read that, for her generation, that was a favourite age for marriage.

As to finding her, it looked a tough assignment. Still, there were quite a few people to whom I could put questions. Some of those questions I might have to put to Dora Marport herself. It was not that I hadn't thought of them till later but because I was far from sure the answers would be reliably unbiased. Still, as I said, a tough assignment. Not that it depressed me. It's always good to have something into which to get one's teeth.

CHAPTER 3
QUESTIONS AND ANSWERS

BERTHA had been busy that morning but what she'd unearthed added nothing to what was contained in that wad of literature. After lunch I settled comfortably down to a re-reading. To assume that Beryl's departure from home was solely due to a resentment of her mother's fantastic absorption in Home and Family was too slick a simplification. Somewhere in that mass of propaganda might be a clue to something vastly different. Clues are like the wind. You can't tell whence they'll come or whither they'll lead you.

By the time I'd had tea I was pretty sure I'd sort of programmed everything into the memory compartment of my private computer. I'm lucky in having a pretty good memory, and an unpredictable one. Often, clean out of the blue, things pop up that I'd thought I'd long forgotten.

But about Home and Family generally. They seemed remarkably well organised: first-class lobbying and supporters in both Houses. The banning of two supposedly pornographic books had quite recently been due to their efforts and they seemed to be the main driving force in the present campaign against television. The next campaign, according to a kind of preview of the forthcoming conference, was to be the drug traffic, with special reference to schools and teenagers.

The Guild also published a quarterly—called naturally *Home and Family*—which gave reports from various branches rather than headquarters. By the way, one other thing was to be discussed at that conference—a proposal to elect a Mother of the Year, with a main and subsidiary awards. That struck me as a shrewd move in popularisation. It was something the Press was certain to report.

Bernice had been busy too. From the friend of a friend, so to speak, she had obtained an introduction to a member, to whom she had represented herself as one on the brink of membership. Bernice herself is pretty well known for good works and she's a remarkably attractive woman. At any rate, the two had lunched together at Bernice's club.

So quite a few more facts were put into the computer. Lady Marport was acknowledged to be the driving force behind the movement, and nobody resented the dominating role she played. She was an excellent and fluent speaker. She was a very wealthy woman but not all of that kind were as generous. The headquarters house in Kelvin Road was one of her gifts and, according to statistics, no organisation spent a greater proportion of its income purely on the purposes for which it was formed.

She was also able to tell me about the late husband—Sir George Marport. It was ten years since he was killed in the hunting field. He was a man of considerable public spirit, having been Lord-Lieutenant of the county and, at the time of his death, still serving on several public bodies. After his death his widow had given Lamington Court to the National Trust, with such of the contents as would cover death duties. Of Beryl Marport, Bernice's informant knew nothing except that there *was* a daughter. Lady Marport often mentioned her in the context of some campaign. "When I think of my own daughter"—that sort of thing.

In the morning I took the car to Wimbledon and tried to time my arrival at Croft House for soon after ten o'clock. It was just over a mile beyond the town in quite a pleasant country road only sparsely scattered with houses, most of them reasonably modern, large and with ample gardens and private drives. Croft House itself was Edward VII "Tudor".

"Mrs. Forster?" I said with my best smile.

"Yes, sir. Will you come in? Her ladyship said I was to expect you."

She was shortish and rather thin. She looked about sixty with hair that was almost grey, and she had that natural dignity that by some sort of osmosis makes distinction of class a rather stupid thing.

She took my hat and coat. "Shall we go through to the breakfast room, sir? It's quite comfortable there."

It was a fair-sized room just through the drawing-room. A lovely fire was burning in the grate and the chintz-covered chairs looked uncommonly comfortable.

"I'm sure you'd like coffee, sir. It's all ready. I'll bring it at once."

The voice was quiet and pleasant with no quaver whatever of age. The room itself was full of lovely things—a Tabriz rug, a French clock with supporting Sèvres vases, and above them what was probably a Gainsborough of two children with a park background. To my left was a superb marquetry bureau-bookcase.

She said she never had morning coffee so I helped myself. I remarked on the room and its lovely things. She smiled.

"You should have seen the old house, sir. When we left we only brought what was needed to re-furnish here."

"Any trouble over staff?"

There was none. Two daily women came in from the neighbouring village and there was also a chauffeur-gardener. We chatted about things like that till I'd finished my coffee.

"Lady Marport told you why I'm here?" I said.

"Yes, sir. You're going to find Miss Beryl."

"I hope I do," I said. "We thought you might be able to help me. She might, for instance, have dropped some hint to you of where she was going."

"No, sir. I was out for that afternoon and evening and when I got back she wasn't here. I went up to her bedroom as usual and I couldn't believe my eyes. All her personal things had gone."

"The chauffeur saw nothing?"

"No, sir. He was working in the kitchen garden. He did think he heard a car but it was no business of his to come and interfere."

"It was very carefully planned," I said. "You had no inkling whatever?"

"None, sir. None at all. It was what they call a bolt from the blue."

"I see. Now I want you to be very frank with me. Even some little thing you may tell me may make all the difference between finding her and not. For instance, were you close to her?"

She slowly moistened her lips as she thought.

"Yes, sir. I think I can say I was. She used to tell me things she'd never have told her mother. Things she'd do in London in the holidays, like going to the pictures or the ballet, or where she had lunch, and once or twice about young men she'd met. She never mentioned names."

"I see. And something even more personal. Was it your opinion that she'd actually begun to hate her mother?"

"Oh, no—"

She broke off. She moistened her lips again.

"Well, what I would say was that she was distant-like with her mother. Except for meals she used to spend all her time in her room."

"I understand it was her father she was fond of as a young girl."

"Indeed she was, sir. She was very fond of riding. She had her first pony when she was only four, but after Sir George was killed she hated everything to do with horses. For a time she was really ill, and then we came here and she was herself again."

"She liked school?"

She smiled. "She loved it."

"And during the last two years have you noticed the gap between her and her mother getting wider?"

She had to think for a moment or two. "Yes, I did. She hated the work her mother was doing. And the thought of being made to do the same things herself."

"She had a will of her own."

"Yes, sir. She was quiet, but you couldn't budge her once she'd made up her mind."

"And just one other thing. Didn't you yourself have to make a complaint about something that happened here with Beryl and her friends?"

"Yes," she said. "I didn't like doing it but I had to. It was one wet afternoon during the last holidays and Miss Beryl brought some friends back from London with her. They came in two cars. There were eight of them: three other girls and four boys: well, almost young men. They had their hair all long like you see everywhere nowadays and they all went up to Miss Beryl's room and began dancing. Miss Beryl wouldn't let me bring up tea. She said they'd all be gone long before her ladyship came home, and then about four o'clock I heard a noise in the dining-room and there was one of the girls and two of the young men helping themselves to whisky from the sideboard. They were very rude when I spoke to them, and when they came out through the drawing-room, a valuable vase was knocked over. That was why I had to report it. Miss Beryl was furious—about the vase, and them, and shortly afterwards they all left.”

“And she’s never had any friends here since?”

“No, sir. Not to my knowledge.” She hesitated. “There *was* one I did hear her mention more than once. A name like Lorry. I think she was a school friend.”

“I’ll remember that,” I said. “But did Beryl ever give you any hint of what she was ultimately going to do?”

She couldn’t help me there. It was clear that she knew what Beryl had no intention of doing, but negatives weren’t of much help. I switched to tastes. What did Beryl do in the house to pass the time?

“Well, sir, she wasn’t in a great deal, except in the evenings during the holidays. I know she used to watch television occasionally with her ladyship. She didn’t have her own set. But she did have a radiogram in her room. She was always playing music.”

“What they call pop music?”

“Yes, sir. And good music too. The piano and orchestras. Good music.”

“The sort that you like yourself?”

She smiled. “Well, yes, sir. I can’t stand that other kind.” She gave a quick look as if she had said something unusual.

I smiled too. “I can’t stand it either. But one last question. You’ve no idea whatever where she may be?”

“None, sir, except that she’s somewhere in London. That’s where she used to go almost every day in the holidays. If she was going early she’d go with Miss Best—”

“Miss Georgina Best?”

"That's right, sir. Harris—that's the chauffeur—used to drive them to Wimbledon and then come back and wait for her ladyship. Sometimes, if she was going later, she used to walk."

I got to my feet. I said she'd been very helpful. "One very personal question. You were fond of Miss Beryl?"

"Yes, sir. Ever since she was born. We had no children of our own, my husband and me, and I got to think of her almost as if she was mine. She's a fine girl, sir. Young lady, perhaps I ought to say. She'd never do anything that was wrong."

I said I was sure of that myself. But had she a photograph of any kind? Lady Marport had told me there were none in the house.

"I've only one, sir. It was when she was on her first pony. A snapshot Sir George himself took and I had it enlarged. I'll get it for you if you'd like to see it. I may as well take the tray with me if you don't mind."

I took a private peep into the drawing-room. It was exquisitely furnished: the sort of place that plays the devil with my morality: that makes me long to come some dark night with a van. In it there'd be the Morland prints, that Stubbs above the mantelpiece, the Bow figures, the marquetry commode that looked like a Peridiez—

May Forster was coming down the stairs again so I went back through the door. A minute and I was admiring the photograph: a small, solemn-looking girl in full riding kit on a shaggy, sturdy-looking pony against the faint Palladian background of Lamington Court. It was a charming picture. May must have caught my smile.

"She's lovely, sir; isn't she?"

"Indeed, yes. A delightful little girl. What colour was her hair? Sometimes it changes as one gets older."

"It's still a light brown, like her mother's. And she still has a lovely complexion."

"Any distinguishing marks?"

There were none that she could think of. I could find no more questions, so I thanked her for the excellent coffee and for all her help. She, too, was a fine person, like the girl she'd quietly defended. She was someone I'd remember for a very long time.

I sat for a few moments in the car, thinking over everything I'd heard and jotting down some notes. One thing of real importance had emerged. When Beryl had left Croft House for good, she had taken all her private possessions. There must have been quite a load—a radiogram, for instance, and a stack of records; books maybe, and certainly the whole of her clothes. If they'd been packed beforehand, May would have been aware of it, so, since they'd been taken higgledy-piggledy, so to speak, they were not going to be deposited at, say, a railway luggage office. They were almost certainly going to a small apartment or a bed-sitter: one that had been secured before the move was made.

Chevrington lay about ten miles north-west of Oxford. I managed to find a route that circled the city itself and brought me out some two miles from the village. I drew in at a pub and by a cheerful fire in the almost empty bar-room, had a pint of bitter with my packed lunch. There was no hurry so I took my time.

The landlady told me where to find St. Winifred's. It was a very high-class school, she said, and all the village ever saw of the young ladies there was on the hockey field which was just back from the road. The school was housed in what used to be the Hall, but new buildings had been added. Quite a lot of village labour was employed.

It was well short of two o'clock when I drove past the lodge along a winding drive. A couple of hundred yards and a sharpish left turn brought me in sight of the main building—a long, early eighteenth-century house, its walls partially hidden by creeper. I drew the car in at the main door. It was wide open.

No one was in sight but I could hear voices coming from the end of the corridor. Then a door opened and a young woman came out. She was walking away from me so I coughed. Her eyebrows were raised as she approached me. I gave her my private card.

"May I see the headmistress, please? And will you tell her it's on behalf of Lady Marport."

She asked if I'd mind waiting. When she reappeared at the end of the short corridor, she beckoned to me. Miss Renwick would see me straight away, she said.

"You knew Beryl Marport yourself?" I said.

"Indeed, yes."

She'd smiled, so I added a little. "A charming young lady."

"Yes, indeed. And very clever. This is Miss Renwick's room. Will you go straight in?"

I tapped for politeness and stepped into the headmistress's study, a smallish room that was practically lined with books and whose knee-hole Hepplewhite writing-desk occupied a lot of space in the alcove of the tall window. She smiled and held out her hand.

"Won't you sit down, Mr. Travers? And do take off your coat. And may I offer you some coffee? Or tea, perhaps?"

I thanked her as I sorted myself out and said I'd already lunched. She had a charming voice and there was nothing of the St. Trinian's about her. She was rather short, on the plump side and probably in the early fifties.

"And how *is* Lady Marport?"

I ventured on a smile. "Very well indeed. As usual, full of good works."

A look of amusement flashed across her face. It might be that we were going to be kindred spirits but I couldn't take a chance. So I told her precisely why I was there. I added—which was perfectly true—that Lady Marport possibly knew I was coming to the school but she hadn't explicitly told me to keep Beryl's disappearance secret. I thought it necessary to be frank.

She frowned for a moment. "I confess I had no inkling that such a thing might happen, but now you tell me, I must also confess that I'm not altogether surprised. Naturally I shall keep it strictly to myself."

I said that was very good of her. But about Beryl. She'd left at the end of the summer term. What was Miss Renwick's judgment of her as she left?

"I may speak freely?"

"Please do."

"Then I was sorry to lose her. I thought her mother was making a great mistake in sending her to a finishing school. Beryl was quite a clever girl and already qualified for entrance to Somerville. That two years would really be wasted. Somerville itself would give her what one might call finishing."

"I'm sure you're right," I said. "Beryl herself almost certainly saw it that way too, which is one of the reasons why she left home. My problem is to find her, and what I'm asking of you is help."

"But how can I help? She never gave anyone here the slightest hint of what's happened. If she had, I'd have heard of it."

"She never told anyone, to the best of your knowledge, what she ultimately wanted to be?"

"Naturally not. She probably wouldn't have been looking beyond Somerville. That's where she would decide."

"Exactly. She'd have to make up her mind what to read. But one other thing. I believe she had a special friend here. A girl with a name that sounded like Laurie."

She smiled.

"Laurie Steevens. They were close friends, as you say."

"Then might I talk with her?"

"I'm afraid you can't," she said. "She, too, left at the end of summer term."

I think I made a face.

"But she lives quite near," Miss Renwick told me consolingly. "At Burgate. You might go through it on your way back to town. If you like I could ring and find out if Laurie is actually at home."

She took a book from the desk drawer and found the number. A couple of minutes and she was talking to, probably, the girl's mother. She cupped the telephone.

"Would you like to speak to Laurie now?"

I vigorously shook my head. A minute or two later she was ringing off.

"Sorry about that," I said, "but if I spoke over the telephone I'd probably have forgotten something I'd meant to ask. Do you know exactly where the Steevens place is?"

She gave me precise instructions and five minutes later I'd left. I hadn't learnt much but I wasn't downhearted. After all, it wasn't often I met two such charming people in the course of such few hours.

CHAPTER 4
THE BREAK

Miss Renwick had assured me that I couldn't miss it, and she'd been right. First to the left past the church and about a hundred yards on and there was Old Mill House, the home of Brigadier and Mrs. Steevens. There was no sign of a mill, but the large pre-Tudor house was there, much as it had always been. Probably a little fortune had been spent on it: the low circular brick wall, for instance, that enclosed the huge front garden: the double garage built to match the house and, just discernible through the elms at the back, a range of tiled buildings.

I didn't like the look of that garage. The doors were wide open and there was no car. A wind had been rising since noon and the rain was spattering against my windshield and I hated the thought of either hanging around till the family should return or making another journey in the morning. But I had to make sure where I stood so I made for the front door.

That rarest of sights these days—a maid in uniform—opened it.

"Could I see the Brigadier?"

"Sorry, sir, but he's gone to London. He won't be back till six."

"And Mrs. Steevens?"

"She's at the Village Hall. It's Women's Institute afternoon, sir."

At least I was definitely in England: there was no getting away from that.

"And Miss Laurie?"

She frowned. "I don't know, sir. If you don't mind waiting a minute I'll go and enquire."

I'd have liked to take a peep at a room but I duly waited on the doormat till she reappeared.

"She's in the stables, sir. Just along the path, there, and round to the left and you can't miss it."

She was right. A bare-headed young woman in jodhpurs and turtle-necked sweater was leading a horse into a loose box. She pulled the horse up when she saw me.

"Do carry on," I said. "I'm in no great hurry."

I waited in the lee of the box till she reappeared. She was a good-looking girl; blond, of medium height and with a carriage that was almost arrogantly erect.

"You're Miss Laurie Steevens?"

"Yes," she said. "And you?"

"My name's Travers." I gave her a card. "I'm here on behalf of Lady Marport, Beryl's mother."

She stared.

"What on earth for?" She stared again. "Has something happened to Beryl? Or is it her mother?"

"Nothing like that," I said. "But is there somewhere we can talk? What about here?"

Here was an open box used as a store place. Trusses of hay made quite good seats.

"What I'm going to tell you is strictly confidential," I said. "Lady Marport hasn't given me any authority to see you. It was my own idea and Miss Renwick's. I've just come from the school. To get to the point, Beryl has left home and it's my job to find her."

"You mean she's run away? Sort of cut loose?"

"Exactly. Perhaps you know she was supposed to go to a finishing school early in September, just after Lady Marport left for America. She didn't. She just collected all her belongings and left. Lady Marport found a letter when she got back just about a week ago saying Beryl intended to live her own life."

"But that's wonderful! I guessed she'd do something like that."

She was looking almost ecstatic.

"It isn't exactly wonderful from her mother's point of view. You do see that?"

"It's her own fault. No one could go on living a stuffy life like Beryl's. If you're a friend you'd know that."

I smiled.

"I'm Kim Travers, the little friend of all the world. At the moment I'm being employed by a mother to find a missing daughter. This is my first day on the job and I'm trying to find out from Beryl's friends and acquaintances if any of them can give me any help. Can you, for instance?"

She frowned. "At the moment I don't think I would if I could. It would depend."

"On what?"

"On the circumstances."

"Fair enough," I said. "You're on Beryl's side. Perhaps I am too, but that's not the point. Sooner or later I shall find Beryl and then my job's done. That also brings us back to where we started from, if you see what I mean. Instead of Beryl telling her mother her intentions by means of a letter, she can tell her to her face—if it matters all that much. So why shouldn't you help?"

She gave a little toss of the head. "I don't think I can."

"When did you last see her?"

"The first week in August. We had lunch together in town."

"And you haven't seen her or heard from her since?"

"No. All that was arranged was that she'd tell me all about the new school as soon as she got there. I was going to Italy, you see, with my parents."

"I see. And did you two young ladies ever discuss what you were going to do with yourselves?" I ventured on a smile. "Except to get married?"

She wasn't tremendously amused. "Beryl wasn't all that interested. She didn't know what she was going to do. I do know that she hadn't any intention of making a career out of that awful show her mother runs. Also I know that when she was younger she wanted to be a ballet dancer but her mother wouldn't hear of it. Now, of course, it's far too late." She gave a little sniff. "That woman ought to be prosecuted for cruelty to children."

"Maybe she is," I said.

She made no comment. I told her the full story and my theory about an apartment. It was news to her: exciting news.

"About other friends," I said. "Do you know any of their names?"

"She didn't make friends. Just acquaintances. People she happened to meet and then drop. I met some of them myself—a frightfully scruffy lot. The sort you'd find in coffee bars or pop dances."

"I see." I hoisted myself up from my bale. "One thing would be of help. Nobody seems to have a photograph. Do you have one?"

She thought for a moment. "Only a house group. Taken just over a year ago."

"Might I borrow it to have an enlargement made? I'd ensure it was returned in perfect order."

"I don't see why not. Shall we go to the house?"

Like most of her class and generation, she was uncommonly sure of herself. I waited in the lounge while she fetched the photograph from her bedroom. There was a huge fire in the open fire-place: everything was comfort and elegance with deeply sprung and cushioned chairs and chesterfield; a sprinkling of period pieces, a Chinese carpet on which it was almost a sacrilege to walk and some fine early water-colours on the walls.

Laurie came down with the photograph. She'd taken it out of the frame. It was the usual school group, about seven by five, and had been taken on a lawn with the school as background. There were thirty-one girls: standing, sitting on chairs and cross-legged on the grass. In the centre of the seated row was the mistress to whom I'd spoken.

"That's Beryl," Laurie said. "The one next to Miss Sands. I'm on the other side."

I had a look at her through my glass.

"It doesn't flatter her at all. You always get a bit peaked off towards end of term."

The face was rather thin. It was an unsmiling face: almost that of a child who waits for the appearance of the little bird. There was something of the Mona Lisa about it, but no smile.

"She was very good-looking, really. Much more attractive than me. And most frightfully clever."

She found some paper and wrapped the photograph carefully up. I didn't say so but it was a pity it hadn't been taken in colour. I thanked her again as I fitted it neatly into my overcoat pocket.

"You've been most kind," I said. "But just one last request. If you should remember anything that might help or happen to hear from Beryl herself, will you let me know? You have my telephone number. After six in the evening would be the best time."

I had intended to complete all those preliminary enquiries that same day calling on the solicitors, but it was already well into the afternoon and what with the deterioration of the weather, and the traffic, I called at the photographer's, then drove straight to the flat and reported to the office from there. Bernice and I were just about to sit down to our evening meal when the telephone went.

"Is that Mr. Travers?"

The voice was a crisp baritone.

"It is," I said. "Who's speaking?"

"Colin Steevens. You called on my daughter this afternoon."

I had a sudden alarm. "I did indeed. You and your wife were out."

"Well, I'd like to apologise for your reception. My daughter might at least have seen you had tea before you left. But about your visit. I've been questioning my daughter about the matter on which you called and I think I've unearthed some more evidence, so may I make a proposition? Could you meet my daughter outside Lyons' Corner House, Piccadilly Circus, at about ten o'clock tomorrow morning? I know it sounds very mysterious, but she'll be able to explain."

"This is all most uncommonly good of you," I told him. "I'll definitely be there."

"Well, I feel a personal interest," he said. "I know both Lady Marport and her daughter. I won't say where my sympathies lie, but I do feel that the information I acquired oughtn't to be withheld. May I wish you luck."

I thanked him and it was he who rang off. I didn't speculate—at least overmuch—about what Laurie might have to tell me in the morning. I just hoped it would be something really to the point. When the time came to do the listening, I was to have one of the surprises of my life.

That next morning I had only about five minutes to wait before Laurie appeared. It was she who approached me: I'd scarcely have recognised her in town clothes.

"What about coffee?" I said. "I know a very nice little place just a minute or two away."

She said that'd be lovely. I said, as we walked, that her father's voice on the telephone had almost scared the wits out of me.

She laughed. "Daddy's bark is far worse then his bite. He's really very clever, you know, at worming things out of people. He's never actually told me, but I think that's his job."

"More power to his arm," I said. "But here we are. It's on the small side but it's really quite nice. And the coffee's good. You like it with cream? Real cream?"

She did. She also ate a large cream bun.

"Now tell me about it," I said. "What was it your father screwed out of you?"

"It was something he remembered," she said. "Something I'd said when I got home after that last time I actually saw Beryl. He couldn't understand why she should go to a business photographer instead of a real one. He didn't say anything at the time but that's what he remembered."

"And last night he got the whole story out of you."

She made a face. "He did. And then he arranged about me seeing you this morning. What you don't know is that he did some checking up on you before he rang. I heard him talking to someone on the telephone."

"Good," I said. "And now will YOU tell the whole story to me?"

It was short and to the point. It was Beryl who stood the lunch that August day and the two said goodbye at Swan and Edgar's Corner. Beryl was taking the Underground but Laurie was staying on in town for an hour or two. She turned into Regent Street, then changed her mind and, when she got back she saw Beryl dodging the traffic at Shaftesbury Avenue and then going towards Leicester Square.

"I know it sounds unpardonable of me but I wondered why she hadn't mentioned anything to me, so I followed her. Then she turned sharp left and went on and on. It was an awful neighbourhood, really—"

"Soho, I think that's where you were."

"It was all new to me," she said. "I wish I hadn't been so nosey and followed her, and then she suddenly went into this sort of shop place. I remember what it said on the front. It was *Marler, Photographer*."

She smiled.

"I thought she was going to have her photograph taken, and then I wondered why she'd come to a crummy place like that. As a matter of fact, I was just going to ask my way back to civilisation, so to speak, when she came out again and there was a man with her—a man with a short beard. He sort of waved goodbye and went back in the shop. I was scared stiff Beryl would see me, so, as soon as she'd gone one way I went the other."

"Most interesting," I said. "She went straight to this photographer's shop, had a quick word and said goodbye to someone who might have been the proprietor. Mind you, she might have had some photographs taken there and was calling to see if they were ready—wouldn't that explain it?"

"Well—yes," she said. "But who'd have photographs taken in a crummy place like that?"

"Maybe you're right," I said. "So let's see if you can find the place again."

It took her a good quarter of an hour to find the place again in Hewett Street, Number 71. It was a smallish shop, its door between two windows, both merely draped. That was unusual. In the window of every photographer you see specimens of his work.

"You stay here," I said. "I'll make an excuse to go in."

I crossed the narrow street. The glazed top of the entrance door had its blind drawn down. There was a smallish card.

Back after lunch

That was all. I went back to Laurie. As I said, now I'd located the photographer's shop, there was no point in either of us waiting.

"What about lunch? You've nothing fixed up?"

"But I have," she said. "I'm lunching with Daddy. I'm supposed to meet him at the Cenotaph at twelve-thirty."

"Then what about coming to my office and having a look at the enlargement I've had made of Beryl?"

She said she'd love that. I managed to get a taxi in Tottenham Court Road. We'd have got to Broad Street far more quickly by Underground but we had plenty of time and it's good for an old stager like me to be for once in contact with an incredibly younger generation.

The six enlargements had just arrived. I gave her one of them and she frowned. It was just the head and shoulders.

"It's not very good of her. It's sort of—well, dumb."

It was certainly a bit stolid. I said I gathered it didn't flatter her. "What colour was the hair?"

"A light brown. Beautiful hair. Much more silky-looking than mine."

"And the eyes?"

She frowned. "I think you'd call them a light brown too. She looks a bit peaked there but really she was awfully good-looking."

I gave her a print. She said there'd be plenty of room in her bag for the original, and then I saw her to a bus which would take her to Westminster in plenty of time. The last thing she asked me was if I'd let her know when Beryl turned up again.

"You promise you'll never tell her how I followed her that day?"

"Finger wet, finger dry," I said. "May I never again have such a charming companion if I tell a lie."

She laughed. She waved to me as the bus moved off, and for some reason or other as I went back towards Broad Street, I was feeling uncommonly lonely.

I rang Bright, Hargreaves and Bright and asked for an appointment early that afternoon with one of the principals. I said I was speaking on behalf of Lady Marport and my name was Travers. It was a couple of minutes before what was probably a managing clerk came on the line. He said Mr. Robert Bright would see me at two-thirty if that was convenient.

Bright turned out to be a middle-aged, rather portly man. Lady Marport had probably consulted the firm about employing us: at any rate, he knew about our Agency. He asked if it was premature to wonder if we'd made any progress. I countered with a right hook. All London, at least, to hunt through and only twenty-four hours on the job. He chuckled.

"True enough," he said. "You've let yourselves in for a remarkably tough job. But what exactly did you want to see us about?"

"To verify the allowance, for one thing. I understand it's three hundred a year."

"Yes," he said. "Up to the age of fifteen it was one hundred. At sixteen it became three hundred and at eighteen it becomes five hundred."

"And how is it paid to her?"

"By cheque. Four quarterly payments. Miss Marport always cashed them at her mother's bank." He smiled. "I rather gather that most of the money was spent on clothes. She always wanted to buy her own."

"The last cheque was sent early in September?"

"Yes," he said. "It was cashed that same week."

"And what are you proposing to do now Beryl has left home?"

He frowned. "Probably send the cheque care of her mother as usual. It will depend on the particular circumstances. After all, it isn't due for some weeks."

"And what would be your attitude if Beryl asked for an advance?"

He shrugged his shoulders. "We'd have to refuse it. It doesn't comply with the terms of the will."

"She might come here personally and plead," I said. "I know you still couldn't grant the advance, but there's something you might do. If she does come, ring our agency and contrive to keep her here for as long as you can. If we could manage to follow her, that would conclude the case."

He said he'd see that that was done. I got to my feet. He looked surprised. "There's nothing else?"

I said there wasn't, unless there was something of which he had thought himself. There was nothing, so we solemnly shook hands.

"I do hope you find the young lady," he told me. "Lady Marport is a very valued client."

He pushed a bell. A moment or two and quite a charming young lady was showing me out.

In the bus that was taking me back to Broad Street I did quite a lot of thinking. At the beginning of September Beryl had received seventy-five pounds, and a further seventy-five wasn't due till the beginning of December. If she had had the idea of leaving home for quite a long time in her mind, then she might have saved more, and the question was if her total assets would have been enough to hire an apartment and to have had enough to live on after paying the first quarter's rent in advance. If she were in ordinary lodgings, then the question of money wouldn't arise.

But somehow I couldn't see Beryl Marport in ordinary lodgings. That I was ascribing to her some snobbery of my own was far from the truth. I just couldn't envisage her in the dullness of a bed-sitter, but maybe that call on the Soho photographer had something to do with it, especially as, according to Laurie, she had stayed for such a short time and the proprietor had seen her off at the door.

What had happened that morning was what I was proposing to find out. But I didn't get back to Hewett Street after all. Bob Hallows was back, and, as there was no job for him on hand, I told him all about the case, and by the time we'd done a bit of arguing, it seemed too late to make a move.

CHAPTER 5
GEOFF MARLER

IT WAS about ten the next morning when I set out for Hewett Street, Soho. Hallows had left earlier. Marler, the photographer, was our only connection with Beryl Marport, and Hallows was to learn what he could from his immediate neighbours. It was a job he could do infinitely better than I. He's unobtrusive and ubiquitous, and, after well over twenty years in the game, he has all sorts of friends in all sorts of places. I'm just the opposite. My height and leanness and horn-rims make me far from inconspicuous, and the only people I feel really happy in questioning belong to the social stratum in which, by the grace of God, I happened to be born. That's not snobbery: it's just a regretful confession.

The door to Marler's premises was open, so I went in, and I found myself in a long, narrow room partitioned into two smaller rooms, the door of each with a glass top. One looked like a waiting room. In it was a table on which were various periodicals, and half-a-dozen chairs. There was no room for anything else. The other was an office with filing cabinets, a couple of chairs and a table on which, among other things, was a typewriter, a telephone and letter trays. A woman's hat and coat hung on a peg in the corner.

In front of me a door with a glazed top opened into a studio. It was large, and what was happening inside had me at first puzzled and then fascinated. Three men and a couple of women were out there in the manipulated lights. A woman of about forty with what was probably a script of some kind in her hand was most likely the absent secretary. The man with a beard seemed in general charge; another was in charge of lighting and the third was the actual photographer. There was a fifth character in this mimed play: a youngish, good-looking red-head who seemed to be demonstrating the merits of a washing machine.

I must have watched those moving, gesticulating figures for another twenty minutes and then suddenly the session came to an end. The red-head disappeared through a door on the right. The four had a brief conference and then the older woman came towards me. I stepped the few paces back. When she came through the door she gave a quick start and then a smile. "Good-morning. Have you been waiting long?"

"Just a few moments. To tell the truth, I was watching what was happening in there. It looked like a demonstration of some kind."

"It was for a brochure," she said. "We do a lot of that kind of thing."

"And you have a woman demonstrator because it's women who'll use the machine?"

"Exactly. We have everything here, including our own models. Had you something of the sort in mind?"

"Not exactly. I wished to see Mr. Marler."

"Then would you like to take a seat in the waiting-room? He'll be free at any moment now."

I'd hardly sat down when Marler did come through. I was on my feet before the secretary could get to her door.

"Mr. Marler?"

He gave me a quick look. "That's right, sir. You wanted to see me?"

"If you can spare me a minute or two of your time."

"Right, sir. Shall we go to my office?"

We went through to the studio. Various rooms seemed to branch off. We made for one to the left, just through the door—a smallish but quite comfortable office.

"You're purely commercial photographers?" I said.

"Yes. Purely commercial. There's no money in the other stuff nowadays except for the big boys." He waved me to a chair. "And now, sir; what can I do for you?"

I'd had a really good look at him. The lounge suit was rather too floridly cut, but it didn't detract from the general air of efficiency. He was about five feet nine, and the somewhat pallid complexion was accentuated by the neat black beard. His speech had the slightest trace of cockney.

I gave him one of our special cards. "I'm a solicitor, as you see, and acting for a lady whose daughter is missing. Her name's Beryl Marport. Do you by any chance happen to know her? This is a photograph of her."

He looked at my card again, then at the photograph. He took far too long over both. "Sorry. Can't help you." He looked up and met my eyes. "May I ask what made you come to me? It seems rather extraordinary."

I shrugged my shoulders. "And you've never seen her?"

"Why should I? If she's some kind of model, then I wouldn't want her. I've two regular models of my own."

"But you *have* seen her," I said. "She called here one afternoon early in August. You saw her. You even went out of the door with her when she left."

For a moment he was rigidly still. His head went on one side as if he was trying to remember.

"Wait a minute. I believe you're right."

He had another look at the photograph.

"You *are* right. This is the one who came and asked if there was a vacancy. What did you say her name was?"

"Beryl Marport."

He shook his head. "That wasn't the name she gave me. I forget what it was but it certainly wasn't that. By the way, would you mind telling me how you knew she'd been here?"

"A friend happened to see her leave with you. This Beryl Marport is quite well connected and the friend was rather surprised to see her in Soho. When we began making enquiries, she volunteered the information."

"Well, sorry I can't help you. Mind you, if I do happen to hear anything of her I'll let you know. Afraid I can't do more than that."

"Very good of you. I'm sorry I've had to waste your time."

"Only too glad to help."

He held the inner door open for me and watched me go through to the street. I glanced at my watch. A few doors along was a tea-room where I had a rendezvous with Hallows and I was a few minutes late. The pavements were pretty crowded and I didn't notice him as he came up. And then I saw something else. The red-headed model was just emerging from Marler's door. She looked at her wristwatch, then set off towards Babington Street.

"That girl," I said. "Let's see where she goes."

She was easy to follow. Where she was making for I had no idea but she ended up not a hundred yards from Tottenham Court Road, in Tempest Street.

COFFEE BAR

The notice, in large lettering, projected above the pavement. The woman went in.

Between us and that coffee bar on the right was a widish turning into Sandown Street.

"Just a minute," Hallows said. "Do you remember Cline and Morgan, the big antique dealers? Didn't they have a kind of warehouse here?"

"That's right," I said. "I remember coming here once."

We took that right turning. That old warehouse had been given a wholly new face. It had been freshly painted and a kind of paving laid in front of the main door. Above that door was large wording in maroon on a black background. A couple of bracket lights were above it, standing well out from the wall.

THE PAINTER ACADEMY

"Academy of what?" I said.

Beyond the entrance doors was another notice affixed to the wall.

THE PAINTER ACADEMY OF
MODELLING AND DANCING
10.0 a.m. to 10.0 p.m.
Enquire Within

"Wonder if the coffee bar's a part of it," Hallows said. "Let's go in and see."

While we'd been following that model I'd told him about my interview with Marler. It's not too easy to explain why you don't trust a man, but he took my word for it. Why I'd suggested following the model was with the hope of getting a private word with her. It wasn't impossible she'd been present that August afternoon when Beryl had called.

Hallows had made an enquiry or two about Marler. He'd heard nothing to his detriment but there was a thing or two, he said, he'd like to follow up. But it was time to go into that coffee bar. It was just as well not to be seen together, so I went in first.

I was enormously surprised. It looked the sort of place to which you could have brought your maiden aunt—spotlessly clean, far from glaringly decorated, and generally comfortable with even a touch of homeliness. A long counter ran the whole length of the left wall, and about half the tall stools in front of it were occupied. The usual apparatus was at the far end. A few shelves displayed cigarettes and boxes of chocolates. Behind the counter a pleasant-faced woman of about forty, in spotlessly white overalls, was using tongs to take a sandwich for a customer from one of the glass containers. He was a middle-aged man and I heard him call her Molly.

I ordered a coffee and a ham sandwich and made my way to one of the tables. There were about twenty of us in the room, and most were youngish. It was peaceful, with only the low chatter of voices. From a couple of speakers high in the walls pop music was drifting over us—and mercifully kept low. People came and went and towards midday the room began to fill up.

There was no sign of the red-haired model, but there was a door in the far wall, so she'd probably gone through to whatever lay beyond, which looked like being the premises of the dancing and modelling school. Then Hallows came in. He took a vacant stool. I couldn't see what he ordered but I heard Molly laugh at something he must have said to her. A moment or two later he began talking to a man on his left.

I'd been there about five minutes when the far door opened and the model came through. Behind her was a man in his early thirties. He was wearing a dark suit and there was something about him that made me wonder if he was the proprietor. His hair and side-burns were black. He was just above medium height and strongly built. Where the counter almost met the door a couple of girls vacated their stools and the model took one of them. Molly smiled as she served her with coffee, then began talking to the man. Her manner seemed to acquire a sudden deference.

Coffee and sandwich, both quite good, were finished and I didn't want a fresh order. But I sat on for a minute or two longer. The man to whom Hallows had been talking got up from his stool. Hallows sat on. Probably he was going to make a lunch of it, for I saw the waitress, Molly, give him another sandwich. Then the dark-haired man to whom she'd been talking turned towards the door. He must have said something to the model for she hastily finished her coffee and together they disappeared through the door.

I didn't feel too comfortable sitting there without making a fresh order, and I didn't want to call attention to myself, so I quietly got up and left. As I went through the door I almost collided with a man. We both apologised at the same time, then he went through and I went out. But he'd given me a quick look as if he'd seen me somewhere before. And then I thought I'd seen him somewhere too. He was tallish; somewhere in the forties, rather ruddy complexioned and with sandy hair. He was wearing a whitish waterproof that was none too clean and a soft hat with a rather full brim.

A cold wind was blowing down the street. I moved on a few yards and stood in the shelter of a door of a delicatessen and waited for Hallows, and all the time I was puzzling my wits and trying to remember where I'd seen the sandy-haired man. Maybe I stood there for twenty minutes and then, when there was still no sign of Hallows, I decided to go back to the Agency. In his own time he'd join me there.

I had lunch at the usual pub and when I got back Bertha said Hallows had rung. He mightn't be back till five. It was nearer half-past when he at last arrived.

*

The first question I asked him was if he'd managed to have a word with that model.

"Never a hope," he said, "but I did find out a thing or two about her. Her name's Susan Farley. She does a bit of modelling in her spare time but her real job is at that academy—old-time dancing. She's an instructress. Here. Have a look at the prospectus."

He took some papers from his breast pocket.

"You tell me," I said. "It'll be quicker."

That academy was on two floors, he said. The upper floor was where the modelling classes were held, and there was also the proprietor's flat.

"Is he the man who came in with the model?"

"That's the one. His name's Painter—Martin Painter. The place has only been open just over a year. I don't know what Painter was doing prior to that but it must have cost him a packet. Everything I saw looked really first class."

"You actually saw it?"

He smiled. "Why not? I went round to the front and asked at the reception desk. That's where I got the literature. The receptionist said I could have a look round, so I did. I didn't see much upstairs because a modelling class was in session, but I saw everything downstairs: a very nice dance floor and cloak-room and lavatories. That coffee bar is for the convenience of patrons as much as the general public."

The other side of the business consisted almost entirely of ballroom dancing. On Tuesday and Friday nights there was an old-time ball when patrons could show their paces. Dress was informal and the hours were from eight till half-past ten. On Wednesdays and Saturdays there was pop dancing with a band, and an extension till eleven o'clock. The receptionist had said it was very popular.

The fee for the pop dancing was seven-and-six, or ten-and-six for a couple. Refreshments were available, which meant the coffee bar. The other fees seemed pretty stiff to me but Hallows reckoned they were reasonable. Overheads came pretty high.

"What about our friend Marler? Anything interesting?"

All he had was some family history. He'd ferreted round till he'd seen an elderly man at the counter of a grocery business and he'd learned from him that Marler's business had been founded by a Conrad Dorne. He was English but his wife was Jewish.

"They both got killed in the blitz," Hallows said. "In Moorgate: that's where they lived. My informant also remembered that there was a son-in-law, a German. My own idea is he was scared when the Jewish persecution began—his wife had Jewish blood—so he managed to get over here, and, when the old couple were killed, he took over the business. His name was Marler. Our Marler's his son."

"He looked in the middle thirties to me," I said, "so that fits in."

"I checked," he said. "That's what made me a bit late. Gottfried Marler was naturalised five years after he got over here. He and his wife both died in 1959, and that's when the son, Geoffrey, took over the business. Previous to that he'd worked with his father."

"And he's never been in any trouble?"

All Hallows knew was what he'd told me. As he said, that chat with the old boy in the grocery business had had to be informal and apparently extemporised. After all, it wasn't worth the risk that word might get to Marler that questions about him were being asked. Also we were not so sure Marler was going to be much help.

"He definitely lied to me," I said. "It rocked him clean back on his heels when I confronted him with evidence that he'd been seen with Beryl Marport."

"Right," he said. "So we keep at him till we uncover something more. Maybe I can think of a scheme to have a talk with Susan Farley."

I was just tidying up that evening in readiness for the meal when the telephone went. Who should be on the line but Marler.

"Marler here, Mr. Blake," he said. "You were asking me this morning about a girl who came here for a job."

"That's right, Mr. Marler."

"Well, I'm sorry I'd forgotten at the time, but her name may have been what you said. Not that I'm actually ringing about that, but something else I've discovered. One of our models, a Miss Farley, seems to know something about her. She'll be working here in the morning and she ought to be free about eleven if you like to come along and see her."

I said that was most kind of him and I'd certainly be there. Supper wasn't quite ready so I rang Hallows and gave him the good news. He didn't seem too excited. Maybe it was just a little too pat. Pat or not, I said I was going to take a chance.

I did. When I got to Marler's place in the morning, the secretary told me he wasn't quite ready. It was ten minutes later when he looked through the door to the studio and beckoned me inside.

There's something I ought to explain. When I hand out one of those fake visiting cards, the name is Blake. The telephone number is my own and so is the address. Should enquiries be made—which has never yet happened—the two hall porters at the flats have been let into the secret of the non-existent Blake.

"She'll be with you at once, Mr. Blake." Marler held out a hand. The gesture took me rather by surprise but we duly shook hands. "Don't keep her too long. She's been working since just after nine."

Before he'd finished speaking she emerged from a room at the back. She was wearing a dark dressing gown and, as she neared, I could see that she hadn't had time to remove all her make-up. The eyes were still heavy with mascara and slight perspiration showed up what was left of the powder. Marler began to fuss.

"This is the Mr. Blake I was telling you about, Susan. You can talk in my office." He gave her a little fatherly pat. "Don't catch cold, darling. Just tell Mr. Blake what you told me."

He left us to ourselves. She led the way to the office. An electric fire made the room almost uncomfortably warm.

"Won't you take a seat, Miss Farley?" I said, and, as usual, tried my best smile. "I shan't keep you long but we may as well be comfortable. Mr. Marler tells me you know a girl named Beryl Marport. Is this the girl?"

She had a look at the photograph. "That's the one. It was me who told her to try Mr. Marler for a job."

"How'd you come to meet her?"

"Well, it was like this," she said. "It was in a Lyons—the one at Charing Cross—and it was pretty full and she asked if the seat next to mine was taken, and then we got talking. She said she had a bit of money but was looking for a job. I only sort of fill in here. Most of the time I work at a place that teaches dancing and modelling, so I was just trying her out, see, when I said would she like to be a model and, when she said she would, I said she ought to take the course. Then she said she hadn't enough money for that but she'd done a bit of modelling and she ought to get by."

"You believed her?"

She shrugged her shoulders. "Well, she had a good figure. Not bad-looking either. I was sorry for her—in a way."

"But there was something about her you didn't like?" Again she shrugged her shoulders. "Well, she was a bit snooty. I suppose she couldn't help it. The way she'd been brought up. School and all that."

"And when exactly *was* this?"

"Just before she came here. At the beginning of August."

"And did she happen to tell you where she was living?"

She frowned. "I think she said it was near Golders Green Station. She had a small apartment and she couldn't afford to keep it on unless she got a job. Oh, and she said she might have some more money in a few months and then it wouldn't matter so much."

"And that was all she told you?"

"All I can remember. To tell you the truth I never thought she'd have the nerve to come here. I didn't even know she had till Mr. Marler told me you'd been asking about her."

"She did tell you her name?"

She gave a little, ironical sort of smile. "She said it was Beryl Martin. Something like that. It was a long while ago and you can't expect me to remember everything. At any rate, I said that wasn't glamorous enough. She ought to have a kind of stage name. And that's what she did. Mr. Marler says she didn't call herself the name you told him."

Two or three further questions produced nothing, so I played what I hoped might be a trump card. You couldn't exactly call it an ace. It wasn't far from a deuce.

"Just between ourselves, Miss Farley, her mother's very worried about her. She suddenly left home and said she was going to make her own way in the world, if you get what I mean. In any case there's a reward of twenty-five pounds, just for locating her. No need to mention it to Mr. Marler, but if she should happen to get in touch with you again—or with him—just ring me. After six in the evening would be best. The number's on this card."

I held the door open for her and watched her cross the studio to what was probably her dressing-room. Marler wasn't in sight but he nobbled me as I was leaving. I thanked him. Miss Farley had been very helpful and I was sure I wouldn't have to trouble her or himself again. He saw me out and my guess was that inside a second or two he'd be in that dressing-room.

As for me, I made my best way back to the Agency. There were quite a lot of things to tell Bob Hallows.

CHAPTER 6
EVENING WITH YOUTH

"I DIDN'T like it," I said. "All the time I had the vague feeling there was something phoney about it."

We were having lunch together at the pub. It was yet another wet morning, and cold with it, but it was snug enough in there.

"Mind you," I went on, "she must have met Beryl somewhere. Where else could she have got the information? That bit, for instance, about coming into some money. Beryl will get five hundred a year when she's eighteen. And about needing a job. If she really has an apartment, then it can't be long before she's hard up. I told you about that. And one other thing. The Farley woman said she'd forgotten all about her till Marler brought up the subject yesterday. Is that feasible? A few days at the most after that chat in the tea-shop, wouldn't she have asked Marler if anyone had been along asking for a job?"

"You'd have thought so."

"Everything was just too pat," I said. "I was told precisely enough and no more. Also I doubt if the Farley woman's as articulate as that. I think Marler did some rehearsing." Hallows wanted to know how I placed the Farley woman. "Well below the lower middle," I said. "There was just the faintest trace of Cockney. She had quite a limited vocabulary."

"What about Marler?" Hallows said. "You had your second look at him."

I grunted. "Still don't know. I still don't like him, but maybe that's a Doctor Fell angle. He was definitely prepared to lie to me yesterday and this morning he was far too ingratiating. And something else. That day in early August when Beryl called on him. If she was what the Farley woman said she was, then all Marler had to do was say, 'Sorry, no vacancy,' and point the way out. Why did he have to go with her through the door to the street?"

Hallows chuckled. "Maybe he's a dirty old man. He couldn't give her a job, but he saw prospects."

"I doubt it," I said. "From what I've been told of her she'd have told him just where he stood, job or no job. There is just one thing. Marler has two regular models. Susan Farley operates in the mornings so the other's on call afternoons and evenings. Is it just possible that Beryl could be that other one?" I liked that theory even before I'd finished outlining it.

"I'm pretty sure Beryl had everything planned well before she made the actual move. She used to spend most of her holidays in town. She could have seen Marler weeks before, and that August call was only to find out if the job he'd promised her for September was still open. That's why she didn't stay long. And why he accompanied her out of the door."

"Sounds feasible," Hallows said. "If so she must have told him the whole story. Then she turned out to be even better than he'd hoped and he wasn't going to give her away, and hence the various lies. He and Farley've been covering up for her."

If that were so, then all we had to do was keep an eye on Marler's premises. Hallows said he'd arrange it.

"What about Golders Green, just in case?"

It was worth at least a try, so when we got back to the Agency, he said he'd fix things up with Norris. It was only then that I remembered something that had been gnawing away at me for the last twenty-four hours. That was why I told him about the man with whom I'd practically collided at the door of the coffee bar.

"Tallish. Sandy-haired." He shook his head. "Can't place him. You can't remember the circumstances?"

"Nothing," I said. "Only him. I've seen him somewhere before and he recognised me. I'm pretty sure of that."

"It'll come back to you," he said cheerfully. I don't know why, but I felt a momentary irritation. That lapse of memory wasn't gnawing at him as it was at me. I hate forgetfulness—in myself, that is. Somewhere, right on the extremist edge of recallment, was the face of that sandy-haired man and with it the circumstances in which we had met. Even more exasperating was the fact that I was sure he wasn't worrying about me. He'd definitely recognised me.

And then another question presented itself. Why hadn't he spoken? If I'd remembered his name, I'd certainly have spoken; then why hadn't he? I could perhaps have found my reasons if Hallows hadn't looked in to say everything was fixed up and he was just off to Golders Green.

I had arrears of work to catch up with that afternoon and just when I was momentarily expecting Bertha to bring in a cup of tea, she buzzed through to say that Lady Marport was on the line. I tell you what happened only because it sounds so utterly trivial. Some days later I was to remember it.

"Ah, Mr. Travers," she said, and paused. "You're sure we can't be overheard?"

"Quite sure," I said. "It's just yourself and I."

"Then I can ask you if you are making any progress."

"It's quite possible we are," I told her. "Believe me, Lady Marport, you'll be the very first to know when there's anything really promising to report. It's a difficult job and we wouldn't try to raise any hopes with optimistic promises. One thing I *can* tell you. It's almost certain that your daughter's still in London, but, as I said before, London's a very big place."

"Yes," she said. "But time's still running away and I can't help worrying. You will let me know as soon as there's anything important?"

"I certainly will."

"Then will you please not try to get into touch with me here. Lines are apt to get crossed, so, if you ring me it must be at my house, and either before ten in the morning or after six in the evening."

She gave me the number. I noted it on the telephone pad and made a covering entry in my note-book.

Hallows rang me at the flat that evening. He'd covered every listed estate agent without any luck. In the morning he was going straight back to Golders Green, this time to try blocks of apartments.

French, the senior operative who'd been assigned to watch Marler's place, reported a minute or two later. He'd had all the luck in the world.

Almost as soon as he'd gone on duty the previous afternoon, a youngish woman with an attractive figure had gone to Marler's place, and the directness, so to speak, of her entry had practically announced that she was working there. Two well-dressed men had entered during the afternoon and had emerged about an hour later. The young woman didn't emerge till just after five o'clock. He followed her.

She walked through to Piccadilly Circus and took the Underground to Holloway Road. Five minutes after leaving the station she was entering a house in Delamere Road: a terrace whose smallish houses now seemed to be converted to double flats. He hadn't been able to see which way his quarry had gone so he took a chance and tried Flat A, the one on the ground floor. A girl in school uniform opened the door.

"Sorry to trouble you," he said, "but does a young lady model live here?"

"You want the top flat," she said. "It's just round at the back there. You'll see the stairs."

"Do you know if Miss—" he made a gesture of exasperation. "I seem to have forgotten the name—"

"It's Yardley. I just heard her come in."

So that was that. A lucky break for once, as he said. I asked him how close he'd managed to get to the model: in the train, for instance. He said he was once so close he could easily have reached across and touched her.

"But she's not the one in the photo. I'm dead sure about that."

"Then bang goes a theory," I said. "But let's check in the telephone directory. She's almost certain to be on call."

In the directory she was: *Yardley, Miss D. Flat B. 27 Delamere Rd, Holloway.*

Just after half-past nine there was yet another call from Lady Marport. She said she was ringing from Croft House.

"I thought I ought to tell you that I've just received a letter—well, it's little more than a note—from Beryl. It's what she promised, if you remember."

"I remember," I said. "But would you mind reading it to me?"

There was no wonder she made no bones about it. It was short and to the point.

Dear Mother,

I promised to keep in touch from time to time. I'm glad to say I'm in wonderful health and quite happy. I've found some congenial work which isn't likely to disgrace the family in any way.

I know this may sound preposterous but if you should decide to give up your work for H and F, you could always let me know through the personal column of the *Telegraph* or *Times*. Please don't regard this as any kind of ultimatum. All I ask is that you should consider it.

Beryl.

"Naturally no address?"

"None. The postmark is W.C.2."

I asked her if she'd do something for me. Would she put letter and envelope in a fresh envelope and with it a set of her own fingerprints? She rather snapped at me when I asked if she knew the procedure.

"You forget that I've had to visit quite a lot of countries."

I asked her to bring it with her to the office that morning. Our Miss Munney would call for it round about eleven.

Bertha left a bit early. She was back at the office before the half-hour.

Dora Marport must have been really on her mettle. A beautiful set of prints—thumb omitted—was enclosed. I got to work on the actual letter and managed to isolate two clear prints that had to be Beryl's. Then I had a good look at the letter itself, and its envelope.

W.C.2 covers a pretty wide area and it was useless as a clue. A few pence expended on a bus ride from where the letter was written could have meant posting in a wider area still. The paper was plain but first-class quality. The writing was bold but neat: letters well-formed and in good alignment.

I was about to put everything into the Marport file when Hallows arrived. He'd decided to abandon that Golders Green enquiry.

"It doesn't mean she isn't there, but you can't do anything when you've only a photograph to rely on. No use looking at a list of names. Heaven knows what name she's masquerading under."

It was a Saturday morning. I said we'd give the whole thing a week-end's rest and begin all over again on the Monday with, I hoped, some fresh outlook. That was after I'd told him about French's unearthing of Marler's second model. He thought it a good idea.

He had a look at Beryl's letter before he left. He also made a joke of sorts.

"Well, we haven't found the lady but we've got her prints. What're you going to do? Send them to Jewle?"

All I could say was that you never could tell.

It had been a blustery day, and soon after our meal that evening rain began driving against the windows of the flat. Bernice hates wind at night: I still find it a kind of lullaby: an emotional hangover from my young boyhood when a howling wind was somehow a reassurance, if only by contrast—the cold world of outside and myself snug in the warm. At the moment Bernice wasn't hearing the wind. She'd acquired the latest book on Bridge and was laying out hands on the card table. Hope, I thought to myself, still springs eternal in the human breast.

I was restless. Television confronted me with at least two hours of ancient hokum, and somehow I couldn't settle to a book. Even if there was my kind of music on the radio, I didn't want to distract Bernice. I also didn't want to think about the case during the whole of that weekend. A clear mind might find some new approach on the Monday, and it was when I was palpably trying to insulate myself, as it were, against everything, that I suddenly remembered the sandy-haired man. I wondered if his connection with that dancing school was just as casual as my own: if, for instance, he'd just dropped in that morning, like myself, for a coffee. A minute or two later I was hoisting myself from the chair. I said there was something urgent I'd forgotten to do. I shouldn't be away for more than an hour.

I put on an old raincoat and a soft hat, and as I was going down in the lift I suddenly remembered that it was a Pop Night at the Painter Academy. To hope to see the man there at all was fantastic enough: to see him when the place was swarming with teenagers was sheer lunacy. Still, I told myself I'd nothing better to do, and the walk would do me good, and out into the night I went. As I rounded the first corner the wind and rain caught me, so I quickened my pace. No walk for me. Two short unfrequented stretches of street and I'd be at Leicester Square Station. A tube to Tottenham Court Road and I'd have only a hundred yards or so to negotiate.

Ten minutes later I was shaking the rain from my hat outside the coffee bar door. Inside were the faint sounds of revelry by night. The room was almost bursting at the seams with teenagers: a mixed lot and hardly so decorous as the handpicked assortments of television shows. All the same there was nothing that even looked like getting out of hand. The fact that Molly wasn't behind the counter was probably the cause. A youngish man in the same kind of white overalls was doing the actual service, but Painter himself was standing at the far end and he didn't look the sort who'd let liberty slip into licence. As I waited in a short queue for my coffee the dull thump of drums and the fainter sound of guitars was coming through the far door. Every time the door opened, the noise was far louder, with the rhythmic shuffle of feet and a strident voice throbbing with ersatz emotion.

I held my cup carefully and looked round for a seat. There seemed to be one at a table for two in the very far corner, so I made a careful way towards it. The seated man looked in the late thirties. He helped me with my cup as I squeezed through to the vacant seat.

"A bit crowded," I said.

"Always is on a Saturday night," he told me. "It's pretty handy for the Tube Station so they come from all-over. Don't think I've seen you here before."

I said I'd been going by and had just dropped in for a coffee.

"What about you? You come here pretty often?"

He smiled. "I'm a sort of chaperone for my young daughter. She's crazy about this sort of thing. I guess all of her age are. But we don't stay on till the end. Half-past ten's quite late enough."

"Indeed, yes," I said. "And you've far to go?"

"Five minutes' walk," he said. "I have a men's shop in Tottenham Court Road. The name's Elwood."

"Just beyond that new supermarket?"

"That's right."

"Then I've been in once or twice," I said. "My name's Blake; I work for a law firm in Chancery Lane."

He held out a hand. "Glad to meet you Mr. Blake. You're married?"

"Yes indeed. Unhappily no children."

"You and your wife dance at all?"

"Nowadays, no. We're just a bit past it."

He laughed. "Don't you believe it. That's what my wife said when I first mentioned about coming here."

He laughed again. "Mind you, I'm not trying to collect any commission. I'm just telling you what happened to us, because after the first night she took to it rightaway. Old-time dancing: that's what we like. You have a few private lessons and then you can come to the dances: you know—the valeta, the two-step, the old-fashioned waltz; that kind of thing. You ought to try it."

I smiled. "Do you know, but you're really getting me interested. What's the actual tuition like?"

"First-class. The whole of this place is—well, superior. It's good enough for anywhere. You might get some bigger, showier places but I doubt if they'd be as good. And it's well run. A bit noisy tonight, but nothing that'll get out of hand."

He was getting to his feet. "May I get you another coffee?"

I watched him thread a careful way towards the counter. I liked him. He seemed genuine as they come.

The room itself was all movement as dancers came and went, and through the quickly opened door came the thump and the shuffling and the maudlin voice. Some of the boys were soberly dressed and some had hair that was reasonably short with only now and again an incipient beard. The dress of the girls was much more uniform, with the hair an almost monotonous sameness. I watched them all as they came and went but there was never a sign of the man with the sandy hair. There were only a dozen or so of us oldsters in the room.

"There we are, sir." Elwood set the cup gently down. "I don't think I spilt any."

"No, no!" I was feeling for some loose change. "Have this on me."

He lighted our cigarettes. I'd forgotten to bring my pipe. The room itself was hazy with smoke, with a faint scent of coffee and the heavier one of perfume.

"It's doing very well, this place?" I said.

"Don't know," he said. "I have an idea Painter's not too satisfied. The last old-time dance the wife and I came to, there were only six couples when the whole floor ought to've been full. Still, it'll probably pick up when the winter really sets in."

"Yes," I said, and suddenly frowned. "Something I was meaning to ask you. The last time I was in here—it was about lunch-time—I just happened to catch sight of a man I thought I knew. A man of about fifty: tallish. Thin, sandy hair."

"Ah!" he said. "That'd be a man called Dorne. He's em-cee-ing the dance in there. Always does on a Saturday night. He's pretty good, so my daughter says. Is he a friend of yours?"

"No," I said. "I just thought I'd seen him somewhere before. You know how it is."

He gave a sort of private nod and leaned confidentially forward. The voice lowered.

"You know Molly Wilson? The jolly sort of woman who's usually at the counter? She and Dorne are said to be pretty close, if you know what I mean."

"Well, it's a free world," I said largely. "Sex is one of the few things we don't pay tax on. By the way, a niece of mine comes here occasionally. I wonder if you've seen her."

I showed him a photograph of Beryl Marport. He had a real hard look at it.

"I think I must have done. There's something about it that's a bit familiar. Nice-looking girl."

A faint hallo reached us from the general noise. A pleasant-looking girl was almost on us. She looked about fifteen. She was wearing a yellowish jumper and a dark-brown knee-length skirt.

"My daughter Nora," Elwood said proudly. "This is Mr. Blake, sweetheart. Been having a good time?"

"Lovely," she said.

I thought I'd better show I was with it. "A good band?"

"Well, a group," she said, and not too reprovingly. "The Hitchhikers. They're smashing."

"You're not going?" Elwood said. "Nora can have my seat while I get some coffee."

I didn't flatter myself that my company had done more than pass the time.

"No, I really must go," I said. "I'm about half-an-hour late already."

"Let Nora have a look at that photograph of your niece. Perhaps she's seen her here."

Nora had a good look. She frowned.

"I don't know. I think I've seen her somewhere." She looked up. "Does it matter?"

I laughed.

"Not a bit. I think she told me she came here occasionally, that's all. It's been nice meeting you, Nora. And you, Mr. Elwood. One day soon I'll be popping into the shop."

"You do that," he said, "and mind you ask for me."

I hadn't prevaricated when I'd said I was late. I'd intended to be home soon after nine but the clock above the counter was well past already. Rain and wind were dead ahead as I made my way towards the station and, once inside, the sudden quiet seemed almost miraculous.

I had to wait five minutes for a train and as I slowly paced up and down I tried to assess the value of what I'd learned from Elwood. There wasn't much to assess, but when I began saying to myself the name Dorne, I remembered, if not too clearly, that Bob Hallows had unearthed the information that the original founder of that photographic business of Marler's had been called Dorne. What that meant I didn't know, and then I remembered something else. That photograph of Beryl Marport had had something in it that was vaguely familiar to both Elwood and his daughter. Maybe that was something that ought to be followed up.

My train came in. A very few minutes later I was getting out at Leicester Square. The wind and rain were behind me as I quickened my pace in the empty stretch of narrowish street. Just round the corner I'd be in sight of the main entrance to the flats. And that's all I remember. That, and a tremendous pain, and a kind of flash.

CHAPTER 7
GETTING THE SACK

WHEN I came to I was lying in the entrance hall. I still don't remember very clearly those first minutes, but I know Bernice was there, and George, the head porter. There were others whom I vaguely saw, but it was only later that I knew who they were.

I'd been amazingly lucky. A very few seconds after someone had struck me, Wayhurst, who has one of the ground floor flats, had seen me lying there. He'd been taking the short way to Leicester Square and had thought, when he'd first seen me, that I was a drunk. Fortunately he didn't pass by on the other side. Even on a night like that, pedestrians are not infrequent and, as soon as Wayhurst had recognised me, he had a small crowd to help carry me the hundred yards to the flats.

Bernice was told and, when she came down, I was lying still unconscious, on one of Wayhurst's blankets with another over me and a pillow under my head. The hospital is only a hundred yards away and, in less than no time, George was back with a doctor. It was just after he'd had a look at me that I had that momentary return to consciousness.

It had been assumed, of course, that I'd slipped up on the wet pavement. That youngish doctor had his own ideas about the contusion once he'd found out from Wayhurst that I'd been lying with my head *towards* the direction in which I'd obviously been going.

At any rate, he assured Bernice that it was safe to move me upstairs. By the morning I'd have a pretty sore head but not much else. In fact it was as I was being taken up in the lift that I really came round. There was an excruciating pain in my head, and, as my glasses were off, everything round me was little more than a mist. But I was remembering just what must have happened.

Bernice found my spare glasses—the others had been smashed—and then the doctor made me drink what must have been a sedative. When I woke it was daylight. The headache was still there but it wasn't too bad until I moved. Bernice fussed round a bit and let me sit up while I drank a cup of tea. Since she knew I'd soon be myself again, she did a bit of scolding: how foolish it had been to go out on a night like that, and how she'd been almost scared to death when she'd first seen me lying in the hall. She wouldn't let me get up. The doctor would decide. He'd said he'd look in round about nine.

That young doctor, as I've hinted, was pretty astute.

"No need to try to kid me," he said. "Someone clouted you. So tell me something. You were sort of leaning forward into the wind?"

I said I thought I was.

"Then that's what saved you," he said. "If he'd caught you fair and square an inch or two higher up, you might be in the mortuary."

"Then don't tell my wife so," I said. "She thinks I slipped up."

"She tells me you run a detective agency," he went on. "You know who did it?"

"Yes," I said. "Someone who wanted to make a quick penny but didn't get the time to clean out my pockets. I checked with Mrs. Travers and nothing was taken at all."

I wanted to know when I could get up. Not before the morning, he said, and then he'd drop in again. Meanwhile a couple of aspirins after a light lunch and a couple more at night would take care of the headache.

Except for a soreness just above my neck and a shooting pain or two if I didn't move carefully, I was feeling almost as good as new by the afternoon. I told Bernice I had to see Bob Hallows. She thought the morning would be time enough, but the urgency I concocted changed her mind.

It was just after four when Hallows arrived: I could hear him talking with Bernice before he came in.

"I'm told not to stay very long," he said. "What's all this about coming a cropper? How'd it happen?"

His eyes popped a bit when I told him the truth: in fact I went over as quickly as I could the events of that evening. I wasn't being dramatic when I said that but for my happening to be leaning into the weather, the blow, from whatever it was, might have crushed my skull.

"Something you're not aware of must have happened at that coffee bar," he said. "But why there? Where's the connection? It's nothing to do with the case. Or has it?"

"Only that Susan Farley happens to work there, and that's not a connection. I think now it's something to do with that sandy-haired man—the one I told you about. He wasn't actually in the bar but he was on the premises and he might have known I was there. He may be wanted for something."

"So he tried to eliminate you." He shook his head. "Sounds a bit far-fetched to me."

He glanced at his watch. "Don't think I ought to stay any longer. Anything I can do?"

I said that if he could think of a safe way of doing it he could possibly get into touch with Molly Wilson. She'd possibly remember him and he might be able through her to find out some more about the sandy-haired man.

"His name's Dorne," I said. "If that isn't some coincidence, he's a distant relative of Marler."

Bernice came in and she had an accusing look.

"Just going," Hallows said.

"And what did you think of him?"

He laughed. "This time tomorrow he'll be right as rain. He just likes lying there and being coddled."

By the time the doctor came the next morning I was feeling practically as good as new and I was sure the doctor was playing it safe. I could get up later in the morning, he said, and have a quiet day. If I felt really fit enough on the Tuesday, I could resume normal work.

"You're telling the police about this?" he wanted to know.

"About what?" I said. "Someone attempted to rob me. I didn't see him. No one saw him. He didn't even have time to go through my pockets before someone was coming and he had a choice of half-a-dozen streets to move off through. So what can the police do?"

He shrugged his shoulders, repeated his instructions and left. You don't keep a dog and bark yourself so I took things easy. I heard nothing from Hallows, but in the morning—except for a slight pain if I happened to move my neck a bit quickly—I was even better than new. I was only half-an-hour late at the agency.

Hallows came in shortly after eleven. He said he hadn't been able to find an approach to Molly Wilson. In any case he thought it too dangerous.

"Someone obviously has it in for you," he said, "but so far nothing's known about me. I think it'll pay for the moment to keep it that way. But I did find out something about our sandy-haired friend."

He'd had half-an-hour at Somerset House.

"It's as simple as this," he said. "Remember Grandpa Dorne who founded the photographic business? Well, he had a son as well as the daughter who married Marler, the German refugee. The son had a son and he's your sandy-haired man. In other words, he's our Marler's first-cousin."

It seemed important, though at the immediate moment I couldn't see just how. I could only theorise.

"So if Marler's really in the know about Beryl Marport, and for some reason or other it's really important we shouldn't find her, then Dorne was the one he'd call in to see I was kept permanently out of the case."

Hallows couldn't see it. What conceivable importance could Beryl have to Marler that he should want me at all costs to be kept ignorant of her whereabouts.

The mooted question wasn't answered. We didn't know it but in a matter of seconds the whole thing was to go up in air. Bertha buzzed through.

"A letter's just arrived by special messenger. I'm bringing it."

I slit open the envelope. The perfectly plain notepaper had the date and *As from Croft House, Wimbledon.* The letter was signed Dora Marport. It took only a few seconds to read.

On my face there must have been a look of utter incredibility.

"What is it?" Hallows said. "Something personal?"

"Read it yourself," I said.

That letter was short and very much to the point.

Dear Mr. Travers,

I have decided after all not to proceed any further in the matter of my daughter. She has chosen to go her own way and, for the moment at least, she must do so. If she should fail to write again as she promised, that may be a different matter.

I am most grateful for what you have done, and now, if you would be so good as to let me have your full and final account, I will at once send you a cheque.

Again thanking you,

Yours sincerely,

Dora Marport.

Clients are always right. We'd known them to change their minds, but never so abruptly.

"It's where we all came in," Hallows said. "Back to square one. If she was worried about her daughter then, why isn't she now?"

It seemed to me that the letter had a hint of postponement and I thought I knew why. That annual conference of Home and Family was getting to be as much as she could, at least momentarily, handle. It was due, I thought, in well under a fortnight.

As I'd said, the client has to be right, but that didn't make the rupture less of an annoyance. When a case begins to get really tough, and when you're far too personally involved, as I'd just been, then it's frustrating to be suddenly called off. The loss of a very remunerative client had nothing to do with it.

"Suppose we do read into it just a matter of postponement," Hallows said, "which means, the way I see it, she'll ask us to take up where we left off. What then? Do we do it?"

I thought we should wait and see. Time to make up our minds if she did approach us again.

He kept plugging away. "Yes, but if she does, and we accept, why not gamble for a day or two? Say the rest of the week. Be ready with a few more facts."

I didn't know. We were far from busy, and, however unrewarding things had been, we might at any moment get a break.

"Very well," I said. "Where do we start?"

To be perfectly frank, we didn't know. There was nothing on which to build except a few ideas, and pretty nebulous ones at that. Most centred round Marler, and what else we could do about him except inquire, maybe, into his private life, was beyond us. There was, of course, the question of why someone had tried to eliminate me, though even there we couldn't be sure the elimination attempt was from the Marport case. Out of that the question arose of concentrating the enquiry on Dorne, the sandy-haired man.

And then I had an idea.

"Look," I said. "Why not get a lot of this done for us? Why shouldn't I decide to tell Jewle about what happened on Saturday night? Give him a kind of anonymous outline of the case. He's bound to make his own enquiries even if they're only personal and private ones."

Hallows agreed. I tried to get in touch with Jewle but he wasn't in, so I left a message with his sergeant. In the middle of the afternoon Jewle himself rang me. Half-an-hour later I was in his room at the Yard.

"Wait a moment," he said, and reached for a writing-pad. "I'd better get some of this down."

Up till then it had been a more or less private conversation: he solicitous at first and then puzzled why nothing had been reported to the police. I tried to prove that, even if reported, nothing could have been done, and then, quite as an afterthought I said it might have had something to do with a case and that's when he reached across the tea-cup for the pad.

"I can't give any names," I said, "but it's to do with the missing daughter of a quite well-to-do woman who was away for a few months and came home to find a letter from this, say, eighteen-year-old daughter to the effect that she was going out in the big world to live her own life. We've been trying to find that daughter."

"But you haven't found her?"

"No," I said. "But we've established the fact that she's in London. It's also possible she's made connections of some sort with Soho."

"How do you know?"

The time had come to mention names. I told him about Marler, and his model, Susan Farley.

"And you're pretty sure both of them were lying?"

I gave him reasons and we moved on to the Painter Academy, where the Farley girl worked. That brought me to the man with the sandy hair. I had to divulge that his name was Dorne and he was Marler's cousin.

"And you thought you'd met him somewhere so you went back there on Saturday night with the hope of seeing him again. But you didn't. He was em-cee-ing a Pop Night. And that's all you know."

It was. He slowly shook his head. "Someone almost killed you. Someone who couldn't possibly have known you were going to that coffee bar. And yet you still think it was because you were there that you were attacked."

"What other reason could there be?"

He gave a little snort. "A far more feasible one would be that someone was tailing you. There wasn't a chance on the way there, but he was ready for you when you came out. In other words, it mightn't have been anything to do with that case you're on. It might have been someone catching up on an old score."

It'd have been bad policy to argue. "All the same I'd be grateful if you could give me some information," I said. "Tell me—not now but in your own time—if you have anything on any of the people I've been telling you about."

He'd given a curious sort of smile.

"Just that," I said. "I'm not asking you to solve a case for me, but if any of the four has anything of a record, it might unearth the mystery of that crack on my skull."

"It might," he said, and wrote the four names down— Geoffrey Marler, Susan Farley, Martin Painter and Dorne. "What's this Dorne's Christian name?"

I didn't know. He said it didn't matter. He'd find out.

"Just one last question. Why didn't that client of yours go to the police?"

"I strongly advised her to before I accepted the case," I told him virtuously. "It was the old story. She didn't want any publicity. I said there wouldn't be any, but it made no difference." That was about all. The talk became chat, and a few minutes later I was on my way back to the agency. As I was to tell Hallows, I'd scattered the seed. All we had to do was wait for the crop.

It was a good thing that we hadn't relied on just ourselves for a continuation of that case. The following night there was a big fire in the Birmingham area. United Assurance were involved and Hallows had to leave in a hurry.

A couple of days after that, Jewle asked if I were free for lunch. I met him at a little place we frequent near Westminster Bridge, and it was during the meal that he told me what he'd unearthed. He said it was purely unofficial so would I keep it in my head. This was it.

Geoffrey Marler—nothing whatever on him. Married with two children. A Harringay address.

Susan Farley—nothing new.

Martin Painter—unmarried. No record but twice under suspicion. Previously ran dance-hall-club in Tottenham.

Query—Where did he get the money for a ten-year lease of those newly converted premises in Sandown St.?

Leonard Dorne—widower. Runs one-man detective agency with small office off Old Compton Street. Once under suspicion for blackmail. Otherwise no record.

It was that last that infuriated me. I ought to have remembered. When we're over-deployed, we hire. There's a kind of pool of free-lance operatives on which the big agencies can draw, and some four or five years back we'd employed Dorne for a day or two on a job which I'd forgotten. That was why I'd thought I knew him and why he'd definitely spotted me.

"He still might have spoken," I told Jewle. "If I'd remembered who he was I'd certainly have said hallo."

"Well, it's one of your suspects eliminated," he said. "And, by the way, I haven't been able to dig deep, but the little I've said is highly confidential and as far as I can go. I don't want any questions from the Higher-Ups."

I was grateful. I even offered to pay the bill but he said it smacked of bribery.

And what use was it all? Exactly none. Somehow without Hallows I lost a lot of interest in the case, and I wasn't prepared to work at it alone. When he came back on the Saturday, he'd lost interest too. What might happen if at some future time we were approached to begin the case all over again didn't seem of any particular moment. As Hallows put it—sufficient unto the day is the case thereof.

PART II
THE GORDIAN KNOT

CHAPTER 8
THAT DAY

I WOKE on a cold, wet December morning with just the prospect before me of another run-of-the-mill day. It was under a fortnight after that letter of dismissal from the Beryl Marport case, which was something I'd as good as forgotten. You might say I was utterly unaware that that particular day was to be one which I'd long remember.

The first surprise came as I was having my mid-morning coffee. Who should ring me but Brigadier Steevens.

"Good-morning, Mr. Travers," came the brisk baritone which I'd heard once before. "This is Steevens. You remember?"

"Indeed I do. Laurie's father. How've you been keeping, Brigadier?"

"Very fit. And you?"

"Still staggering along," I said. "And how's your charming daughter?"

"Ebullient as ever. By the way, she sent you her love, whatever that amounts to."

I had to smile. She was a delightful girl.

"It's like this," he went on. "You and I have never met, but what about lunching with me this morning at my club?"

"That sounds fine," I said. "The only thing is I consider I owe you the lunch. So why not make it at my club?"

He said he'd be delighted, so I gave him directions.

His taxi was dead on time. He was a fine-looking man in the late fifties, well-preserved and rather on the lean side like myself. His face was well tanned and the black hair was just beginning to go grey at the temples. We shook hands and surreptitiously sized each other up.

We had a preliminary sherry. I'd managed to secure a separate table and we'd hardly got ourselves seated when he was asking how the search for Beryl Marport was coming along. I'd promised, you may remember, to ring Laurie as soon as there was anything to report.

There was no reason to be other than frank about at least the little I was prepared to tell him, which was that the axe had fallen at the root of the tree.

"Called you off?" he said incredulously. "A pretty callous thing to do, wouldn't you say?"

I shrugged my shoulders. "Beryl's her daughter. Also it's quite possible that I wasn't given all the facts. Lady Marport's a very astute woman."

He grunted. "She's over-bearing and damnably self-centred. Beryl wasn't a daughter. She was something to be manipulated. The worst kind of matriarch."

I said it certainly looked like it. It was in the holidays that Beryl had found life particularly boring. Apparently she'd been happy enough at school.

"I'm with you there all the way," he said. "It's a fine school. Uncommonly well run. The headmistress is a remarkably gifted and dedicated woman. A bit on the advanced side but none the worse for that."

"In what way?"

"Well, she didn't run the place like a nunnery. Take the weekly winter dances for the senior girls. Suitable partners used to be asked from the colleges. Laurie used to enjoy it no end. And they were allowed to attend the local annual Hunt Ball. Then there was the science side. Not the old frog-dissecting our wives had to perform but the real thing. I hear they're even about to install a small computer."

"Good luck to them," I said. "And speaking as one who's not too young to remember the suffragettes. But I'm glad you told me that. I seemed to have guessed right when I said she was happy at school."

"She's a fine girl," he said. "Between you and me, she deserves a damn-sight better mother."

Something he'd said a second or two earlier had given me a sudden idea.

"This is purely an academic question since I'm off the case, but couldn't Beryl have struck up an acquaintance, or even something more, with a boy from one of those Oxford colleges?"

He looked a bit startled. "Didn't think of that. You might just be right. I'll have a word with Laurie and give you a ring." His eyes popped again. "Good God! She might even be married! Wait a moment, though, she's well under age, so wouldn't she have to get her mother's consent?"

I agreed that she would.

"Could she have passed for twenty-one?"

"I think so," he said. "Girls mature pretty early these days. Plenty of them marry at eighteen."

"If she *is* married," I said, "that might partially explain things. Or does it? I know she has either to be married or to come of age before she can get what her father left her. But if she is married, then she's almost certainly living somewhere in town."

No names, no pack-drill, so I gave him just a rough idea of how we knew. And that was about all the conversation we had concerning the Marports. We somehow slipped into reminiscences of War House futilities, which was much more amusing. Then when lunch was virtually over, it turned out that he had to get away. Just time for coffee at the table and then I was seeing him off. He reminded me that he'd be giving me a ring. I said I'd almost certainly be at home, and gave him a private card.

I'd enjoyed the meeting. It was nice to think that as soon as was convenient for both of us, we'd be seeing each other again.

It was not yet two o'clock when I got back to my office. I wasn't feeling like work for the moment so I got my pipe going and tried to get those lunch-time reverberations of the Marport case out of my system. Then the buzzer went.

"A Sergeant Harries wants to speak to you, sir."

By the time he was through I hadn't succeeded in placing him.

"This is Detective-Sergeant Harries, sir," the voice said. "Something urgent has turned up, sir, and the Super would like to see you."

"Chief-Superintendent Jewle?"

"That's right, sir. A car's practically on its way to pick you up. That all right, sir?"

"I'll be here," I said. "But—"

The line went dead. I gave a dry smile. Things *were* urgent, and it was no use guessing what on earth they were. I had a word with Norris and put on my overcoat and waited outside. Ludovic Travers. On the alert and always ready to co-operate.

I waited a good ten minutes out there in the blustery cold before the car drew up. Harries—I remembered I'd seen him when I'd last been at the Yard with Jewle—had the door open, and I'd hardly dropped back in the seat before the car was off again.

"Where're we bound for, Sergeant?"

He smiled. Don't ask me why. "Along the river, sir."

"Good," I said. "And when do we embark. And for what port?"

This time he chuckled. "Just driving along the river, sir. Shouldn't be more than ten minutes or a quarter of an hour."

I didn't ask any more questions. Once we'd left Bishopsgate I was in strange territory. All I knew was that we were never far from the river. Now and again the masts and cranes and even funnels were only a stone's-throw away and then we'd turn slightly inland again. And then suddenly we slowed. A sharp left-turn and we nosed our way along what was more of a passage between warehouses than a street, and the river lay just beyond.

The car stopped. Harries reached across and opened my door. The noises of the port were suddenly all round us.

"This way, sir."

I followed him. We turned left again. Ahead of us two police cars were drawn up alongside what I guessed was one of the headquarters of River Patrol. We turned right into the comparative darkness of a covered space. Harries motioned me up the steps. As I reached the landing, Jewle appeared through an open door.

"Good of you to come," he said. "This way."

He motioned me forward into quite a large office. A huge bay window overlooked the river. In the space before it was what was probably a body, the trestled planks making a kind of bed. A uniformed sergeant joined us from behind the desk. It was he who drew back the blanket.

"You know him?" Jewle said.

I'm squeamish about corpses. I've said it before and I say it again. Some, especially when fished from the river, can be far from pleasant sights. But this one wasn't. There was nothing repugnant about the man who was lying there. The only odd thing was that he was stark naked.

The head was sideways. Jewle reached forward and moved it.

"Recognise him?"

I didn't need a long look.

"Yes," I said. "It's Dorne. The one I called the sandy-haired man."

"Dead sure?"

"Dead sure," I said, and didn't mean it for a joke.

The brief tension suddenly went. Jewle introduced me to the sergeant.

"Tell Mr. Travers what happened."

"Nothing much to tell, sir. We spotted him about half-past twelve and fished him out. Him being naked made him easier to spot. A couple of hundred yards up-stream when the tide was almost out."

There were steps outside and in came another old friend—Doc. Anders. We might have been meeting in a pub, the way we greeted each other.

"Take a good look at him, Doc.," Jewle said. "You can have an even better look later when we get him to the mortuary."

Anders flicked off the blanket and got to work. I didn't look. I filled my pipe and got it going. To everyone else in that room corpses were ten a penny: to me they're a sudden reminder of mortality. Take them away and just as suddenly they're something academic: something one might have read about in a paper: a reason for enquiry and the search for an answer.

"Not more than a couple of days," Anders said. "May know more when I look inside him."

"And the stab wound?"

"What about it?"

"How long before he was chucked in the river?"

"What d'you want? Miracles?" Anders was a cantankerous cuss at times. "Get him along to the mortuary. And don't expect any quick answers."

Jewle shrugged his shoulders. "Right then. You see to everything, Sergeant. And let me have a full report. Might as well get along."

That last was to me. He drew back to let me go ahead down the steps.

"Might as well go back in my car," he said. "Think we could set you down at Broad Street. We can chat on the way there."

"Why not?" I said. "There's a whole lot of things I'd like to know myself."

We'd only just moved away when he was making a further suggestion. It would be handy for me if I were dropped at Broad Street, but why shouldn't both of us talk things over there? I told him it suited me fine.

Bertha brought in some tea. There was no hurry. It wasn't the first corpse that had been fished from the Thames and it wouldn't be the last. It had been identified and now Jewle had it, so to speak, on his hands. It was a case of murder, but you still gained nothing by rushing around.

"Looks as if you're in this right up to the ears," he said. "You think you could lend an occasional hand?"

That was just polite flummery. He knew well enough it'd be harder to keep me out than ask me in. Not that I didn't think I'd have something to contribute. In fact I was contributing already. As soon as we'd stepped into my office I'd made for the files. We have an elaborate cross-reference system and it didn't take more than two or three minutes to find the name Dorne.

"Here he is," I said. "March 1952. He was living at that same address in Ferris Street. We used him for five days and paid him for a week. The job was tailing a man suspected of fraud."

"How does a man get in what you called the pool?"

"It's easy," I said. "A small man has slack times so he goes to a big agency and says he's free if they should need a man at any time. His credentials are examined and he's probably in. If we want an extra man urgently we ring another agency. They mayn't have a man to spare but they'll suggest ringing So-and-so. In this case we rang Dorne."

"In other words, you were satisfied, or someone like you was, with his credentials at that time."

I said that was so. I also said that we must have been satisfied with him because, though we'd never had any reason for complaint, I'd certainly have remembered his name if there had been: even though it was four years ago.

"And you haven't employed him since?"

"Couldn't have," I said. "No entry."

"Then there's something I'd like you to do," he said. "It'll come better from you than us. Get hold of the agencies you usually ring and find out what they have on him."

It was a job that Norris would be glad to do. Then I had a question of my own.

"I didn't see the actual wound, but Dorne was stabbed?"

"In the back," he said. "At a guess, I'd say with a flick-knife. Almost certainly pierced the heart."

"And whoever did it didn't want identification, which was why he was naked."

"That's it; and then he was dumped. It might have been straight in or from a boat." He gave a wry smile as he noted that in his book. "Nice and handy if he has friends who go in for that sort of thing. And what about friends?"

I reminded him there'd probably be plenty at Painter's place. Then there was what I'd been told about the waitress, Molly Wilson. She and Dorne were said to be pretty close.

He made a note.

"And now to the thumb-screws," he said. "You ran across Dorne again because you were engaged on a case, and you were where you were because of that case, so I want to know all about it. Strictly between ourselves, of course, but I want names and the whole thing as far as you'd got till the night you were coshed. It may be long odds against Dorne being involved but I'm not taking any chances."

I thought it over while I stoked my pipe.

"We're no longer on the case," I said, "but the files are here. This one isn't complete but it's detailed. If I leave it over there by your overcoat, you could pick it up when you leave. That'll satisfy what's left of my conscience."

He laughed. Other people's consciences don't keep him awake much at night. He did say he'd see it was kept strictly confidential. As soon as he was satisfied the killing of Dorne had nothing whatever to do with what was in that folder, then he'd personally return it.

He got to his feet. "I think that's about all. If I have to use you people, you think you'll be free?"

It was my turn to smile. "I'm free myself. Bob Hallows will be in the morning, so it's just a matter of fees."

He made a rather ponderous joke about bloodsuckers and then I helped him on with his overcoat. He managed to get that none too slim file into a pocket.

"You'd like Anders' report?" he said. "If it doesn't come through too late, I'll give you a ring. And what about the morning? You think you could come along about ten?"

I assured him I'd be there.

Brigadier Steevens rang soon after the evening meal.

"That matter we were discussing at lunch," he said. "Laurie has an idea we may be right. At any rate there's an Old Girls' function of some sort this coming week-end and she's going to make some discreet enquiries. If anything comes out of it she'll get in touch at once. That all right?"

I said it sounded most promising.

"That's what I thought. Thanks again, by the way, for an excellent lunch. And your company. And don't forget I'll be ringing you as soon as I get back from Germany."

The next call came just before I was thinking of bed.

"Just read the preliminary report from Anders," Jewle said. "He now thinks the period of immersion may have been up to three days. That takes us back to, say, early last Sunday. Easily the best time for dumping anything in the dock area. Also I was right about the flick-knife. That or something like it. That mayn't be all, of course. The back-room boys haven't had their fun and games yet. Let's hope they find something. Not much to chew on so far."

I thanked him and said I'd be seeing him in the morning, and that was all, except to take that afternoon's happenings to bed with me. I may have said it before but it takes me quite a time to get to sleep. Or it did take me till I found my own anti-insomnia remedy, and that's to begin thinking of something pleasant as soon as my head has warmed the pillow. It may be a television programme I've chanced to enjoy, or a book I've been reading, and now and again I go back a few years and replay one of my happier rounds of golf.

That night I began by asking myself how Dorne could possibly have had any connection with the Beryl Marport case, and almost at once I came up with some sort of answer. It was in Painter's place that I'd first seen him. He'd looked almost startled at the sight of me but he hadn't spoken. And why had someone attempted to kill or badly incapacitate me that Saturday night if it were not because my presence in that coffee bar had been considered dangerous?

I could find no other reason. Someone didn't want me in that bar again. But why? And where did Beryl Marport fit into things? Another moment or two and I had a fantastic idea.

Suppose Susan Farley had been lying, as I'd indeed suspected. What if Beryl had told her the whole Marport story? And that story had got round to Painter. Painter might have had a word with Dorne.

"Look, you're a detective. Check up on everything."

Very well, then. Dorne found the story to be true. And the outcome, much later, was kidnapping!

Fantastic? Well, there it was. And there were two things that seemed to back that theory up. In fact there were three.

A kidnapping would account for that sudden terminating of the case by Beryl's mother, and out of that emerged two more things: Beryl's whereabouts had been divulged and the kidnappers had been paid off. The ransom money must have been pretty hefty but there'd been a quarrel over who had how much, and that was why Dorne had been killed. And why care had been taken to make him disappear without trace. If ever anything got out, then it was the dead Dorne who might emerge as the sole agent.

I liked all that. In the cosiness of the bed it seemed more and more plausible, and there was a third thing that made it even more so. Why, for instance, had Jewle wanted the whole history of the Marport case if he hadn't had ideas that coincided not too distantly with my own?

It was that pleasurable deduction that I remember last. When I woke in the morning things didn't look quite as rosy. I was getting out of a warm bed, not still in it, and it was yet another rainy day. Hallows was back at the agency and I spent a half-hour bringing him up to date. He listened politely to my overnight theories but maybe they weren't presented with too much fervour: at any rate, he listened and no more.

"I'll get on with ringing the agencies," he said. "I take it the idea is to find out if everyone always found Dorne to be perfectly straight."

Jewle wasn't in his room but Harries said I was to wait. He ought to be back at any minute.

"Nothing in the paper this morning about our friend the corpse," I said.

Jewle must have been bringing them up very tight-lipped.

"Not yet, sir. Something's going out this morning. Just a corpse taken from the river, and suspected murder."

CHAPTER 9
Social Calls

Jewle said he'd practically finished with the file of the Marport case but might he keep it for a day or two longer. He'd like to go through it again.

I didn't mention those theories of mine, and in a couple of minutes I was glad I'd kept my mouth shut. What I did ask was if he'd found a connection with the murder of Dorne.

"I don't know," he said. "Something's there, but I just can't get hold of it."

"Something was missing?"

"No," he said slowly. "But let's leave out Dorne and take it as you did—from the Beryl Marport angle. She called on that photographer, Marler, asking for a modelling job, thanks to the good offices of Susan Farley, but she didn't get one. But you think Marler and Farley didn't tell you all the truth and I'm inclined to believe it. What I do think is that Farley told her employer, Painter, all about it. The daughter of a wealthy woman estranged from her mother and living alone. Quite romantic, though maybe Painter didn't see it that way. Maybe he saw possibilities—"

"Blackmail?"

"Could be. Our people are still wondering where he got the money from to buy a lease on the place he's got now. So Farley was asked to modify her story a bit and to ask Marler to do the same."

"But where does Dorne come in?"

"Well, he was a pal of Painter's and a private detective, so Painter asked him to verify Beryl's story. Find out if her mother was really wealthy and so on. That'd take time."

"Mind if I have a shot at the rest of it?" I said.

He waved a hand and told me to carry on.

"Then what I'd have done would have been to find Beryl a comfortable job somewhere and keep her stashed away till some sort of blackmail scheme'd been worked out. I don't know what kind of scheme, but I do think it made Lady Marport give us the boot. And that it was successful and that there was an argument over the money and that someone, not necessarily Painter, stuck a knife in Dorne's back."

"Interesting," he said. "As a matter of fact it isn't so far off what I got to thinking myself; also I went a bit further. The one way they could have got money out of the mother was by offering to tell where the daughter was, so, unless there was some double-crossing, your Beryl's now back at home."

Things were beginning to fit in.

"Why not try it out?" I said. "Inside ten minutes we could know one way or the other."

I outlined the plan. He pushed the buzzer for Harries. It took the ten minutes to get the plan rehearsed. When Dora Marport was at last on the line, Harries was handed the receiver. What Jewle and I heard was something like this.

"Good-morning, Lady Marport. I'm Peter Devonshire. You may have heard Beryl mention me. I've been away for some time but I'd like to see her again. I gather she's not at Wimbledon, so could you tell me where I could contact her? . . . On a holiday? . . . Yes, but Lady Marport, could you tell me where exactly she is . . . I'm very, very sorry. Will you tell her I rang?"

From the rather blank look on his face we gathered he'd been cut off.

"She says she's away," Harries said. "Recuperating after a slight illness."

"Could be," Jewle said, but didn't look too convinced.

I had another idea. A minute or two and I was through to Croft House, and that delightful old housekeeper, May Forster, was on the line. A few polite words and I was asking a couple of questions.

I thanked her and said I was very grateful. And she would keep our little talk to herself? It would be in Beryl's own best interests.

"There we are then," I said to Jewle. "That housekeeper's been in the know about Beryl all along, and if she says Lady Marport still has no idea where Beryl is, then we can take it as gospel. Which means, if our theories've been right, that she was double-crossed. Cash paid out but no Beryl."

"Looks like it," Jewle said, and got to his feet. "About time we started paying a few social calls."

I must have looked a bit startled. He laughed.

"Not on whom you think. Having a look at Dorne's place. No need for a warrant. I don't think he'll mind."

We came into Ferris Street from the Shaftesbury Avenue end and parked the car behind an unloading van. Mayne House was only a few yards on. Jewle had done a little legpulling. Dorne and I were both in the same profession so I might spot something which he, Jewle, could easily overlook.

Mayne House was an out-at-elbows, Victorian, three-storey block and, judging by the list of tenants just inside the entrance, a rabbit warren of smallish offices. L. Dorne, Enquiry Agent, was on the first floor. We didn't see a lift so walked up the bare stairs.

The lettering on the frosted glass was rather worn— LEONARD DORNE PRIVATE ENQUIRIES Please ring.

Bob Hallows is the best man I know at manipulating Yale locks, but Jewle wasn't bad. Half a minute and the three of us stepped inside. We stood there, taking a slow look round. The room had a clammy kind of chill.

Straight ahead, in what had originally been a fire-place, was a small electric heater. On the mantelpiece above was a metal alarm-clock and by it a telephone. By the left wall was a green, chipped filing-cabinet with what looked like a cupboard to its left. To the right was a Victorian, knee-hole, mahogany writing desk. A worn swivel chair was behind it with the light from the one window coming across conveniently from the left. The shabby, wall-to-wall carpeting was worn almost to the jute from years, maybe, of tread from door to desk. To the right were two spare chairs and a four-foot repro-duction china cabinet with three of its shelves untidily stacked with books. Through a half-opened door to the right of the fireplace could be seen part of a wash-basin.

"Looks as if no one's been here for a few days," Jewle said. "See that film of dust on the desk where the light catches it? Wait a minute, though. See the smudges?"

Someone had gone through that desk, and quickly. Three of its side drawers weren't properly closed. In one drawer were a couple of empty whisky bottles. Two of the others had oddments of correspondence, two or three old newspapers and some cuttings.

On the desk top was a stationery holder with plain paper and envelopes; an indelible pencil and a couple of ball-point pens in its tray. Nothing else but smudges in the thin film of dust.

"Whoever was interested was wearing gloves," Jewle said. "Wait a minute, though."

Transversely, as it were, across the very front of that desk as we looked on it, were two smudges with a trace of prints, one each side of the knee-hole below. It took a minute or two to work out just why they were there.

"Someone was steadying himself while he looked underneath," Jewle said. "Get under there with your torch, Harries, and see if there's anything else."

Harries wriggled in on his back. Half-a-minute and he was wriggling out again.

"I think you ought to have a look yourself, sir. Looks to me as if something's been stuck underneath."

Jewle's shoulders were too broad but he got one shoulder in. A second or two and he was asking if either of us had a halfpenny. Harries had one. There was a grunt or two from beneath and Jewle wriggled clear.

"You were right. Something was stuck underneath. Probably with cellophane. Something about six by four."

"Like a bundle of letters?"

"Could have been," he told me. "Whatever it was, it's gone. Later on we'll get the whole thing photographed. Turn it up on its side."

"Why one hand gloved and another ungloved?" I said.

"Don't know," he said. "I think there were two different people here. One was having a general search and the other wanted what was taped down. Let's see what else there is. Mr. Travers, you go through those books and, Harries, you have a look at that wash-room."

With my gloved hands I carefully shook out each of those books. They looked to me like a job lot from Charing Cross Road bought to impress Dorne's clients. Two or three of the paper-backs were fairly new, the rest pretty old, but at least two were strictly business— Glaister's *Medical Jurisprudence, Toxicology and Public Health* (1902 Edition) and Dr. Hans Gross's *Criminal Investigation*, of 1949.

I was easily the last to finish. Harries said the small room was merely a wash-room closet. Empty toilet roll and a torn *Daily Record* in its place. The electric fire was in order but the telephone had apparently been cut off. Quite a few telephone numbers had been pencilled on the wall-paper just above.

I saw the cupboard for myself. A folding bed stood against the back. On the floor were a kapok-filled mattress, four greyish blankets and a couple of none-too-clean pillows. From the general mix-up it looked as if that cupboard had been searched. As for the filing cabinet, there was nothing in it. It, too, may have been bought for show.

Jewle took a quick look at his watch. It was already half-past eleven by mine.

"Right," he told Harries. "Write this down. I want the room printed and photographed, even the smudges. The files of the likely Sundays are to be gone over to see if Dorne advertised and, if so, when was the last time. Every tenant's to be asked if he saw anything suspicious, on, say, both Saturday and Sunday last. Find out if there's a caretaker, on Sunday night. And possibly Monday. You got that?"

The door was left just ajar. Jewle and I went down to Ferris Street.

"Where now?" I said.

He didn't go back to the car: just took another quick look at his watch.

"Don't know about you but I could do with a cup of coffee."

I said the Corner House was only just three minutes away.

"A bit too crowded for me," he said. "Think we'll try something a bit more Old School."

That was when I guessed he'd intended all along to go straight to the coffee bar at Painter's place. Jewle has his own kind of joke: one with a built-in, delayed action sort of mechanism.

It wasn't all that distance away, and, between dodging pedestrians, we talked chiefly about Dorne's office. Our judgment was that he hadn't used it for maybe the best part of a week. It was plain, too, that he'd often used it as a bedroom. There'd been cleaning apparatus in the wash-room, so maybe he tidied it himself. If not, then the caretaker might know about it. Offices like that often shared a cleaning woman.

One thing Jewle didn't want—too much and too early publicity. Once he'd got all he needed from that office, it wouldn't matter so much. Publicity's always a tricky decision. It can help and it can harm. As the text-book says, what counts most must always be the interests of justice.

He knew far more than I'd thought about that Painter Academy. We stood for a moment or two in Sandown Street, looking at the front.

"Smart-looking place," he said. "Painter had to cough up fourteen thousand for the ten-year lease. Then there's the ground rent."

He was moving off but I held him back.

"Suppose what we talked about this morning was true. Lady Marport couldn't have paid all that much just to learn the whereabouts of her daughter. If the money was split, all Painter would have got was, at the most, a hundred or two. What good was that to him?"

"Don't know," he said. "It's the Fraud Squad who're interested in his money. We're just a subsidiary."

We entered the coffee bar. Only about a dozen customers there. Molly wasn't behind the counter. In her place was the youngish man who'd been there with Painter the night I'd been attacked. I did the ordering.

"Two coffees, please. Ordinaries."

I paid. While he was getting my change, I asked what had happened to Molly. He shrugged his shoulders.

"Taking a day off, I guess."

I left it at that. We took the coffees to the back. Jewle's not much of a smoker but he lit a cigarette. I stoked my pipe.

"Clean little place," he said. "What're things like inside?"

I said I didn't know. I'd never had the chance to look.

"Soon as we've finished these, we'll find out," he said. "Where're the lavatories here?"

"Probably through that door. Again, I haven't had a chance to find out."

"Give it a try," he said. "I'll stay here."

The man at the bar nodded back and said just through there. I went through to a sort of vestibule, all nicely tricked up with coloured windows, a tessellated floor and a couple of huge potted palms. A lavatory was on each side. I tried the through door but it was locked and I couldn't see through to what was probably the dancing floor because of the frosted glass of the stained windows. The *Gents* I used was spotlessly clean.

I'd already drunk my coffee. Jewle had finished his by the time I got back to our table. I gave him the lie of the land and we got up.

"Time to throw a little weight around," he said. "Let's try the front."

The front doors opened into a smallish office. A good-looking, dark-haired secretary-receptionist was sorting some correspondence at an almost new, fumed-oak desk. She looked up and smiled.

"Can I help you?"

"Perhaps, yes." He gave her his Warrant Card. "I'd like to see Mr. Painter."

Half a minute later she was showing us through. That dance floor was even bigger than I'd thought. By the left wall was a raised platform: to the right a smaller one, and circular. To our near left were the stairs.

"We'll find our own way now," Jewle said. "You just tell us where Mr. Painter is."

We waited at the foot of the stairs. Half-a-dozen chattering girls were coming down: good-lookers, all of them. Probably a modelling class. When they'd gone we went up to a wide landing. At the beginning of one passage a notice said STUDENTS ONLY. We took the other. It led straight to another door.

OFFICE
Please Knock.

We knocked. A sound from inside seemed an invitation to enter. We were in the right place. Painter rose from behind his handsome desk and held out his hand. Jewle duly shook it. "This is a surprise, Superintendent."

He gave me a look but didn't hold out his hand. "Haven't I seen you somewhere before, sir?"

"You have indeed," I said. "Now and again I patronise your excellent coffee bar."

He waved a hand. "Sit down, gentlemen. Might as well be comfortable. A cigarette?"

We declined. He lighted one for himself. He was younger and far better-looking in that bright, quite cheerful room.

"Nothing serious," Jewle said. "We were just wondering if you could help us. The one we really want to see is a Leonard Dorne. I believe he works for you."

"Occasionally, yes," he said, and, as far as I could see, he hadn't batted an eyelid. "Usually on Wednesday and Saturday nights. He em-cees the Pop Nights. He's a pretty tough character. Sees things don't get out of hand."

"When did you see him last?"

"Saturday. Why? Is anything wrong?"

"Don't know," Jewle said. "We've just been round to that office of his and he isn't there."

Painter leaned forward. He almost wagged a finger.

"Look, Superintendent, if he's wanted for anything serious I think I ought to know. I mean, I couldn't go on using him here. We've got a good reputation."

"Nothing's proved as yet," Jewle said. "Just a complaint from a former client. Naturally it's got to be investigated."

"Of course," he said, and leaned back. "Nice of you to let me know. Naturally I'll keep it to myself," He frowned. "But I didn't gather he'd been doing much work in that line lately. He was doing pretty well up to a year or two ago and then things went slack. That's why he was glad to come and work for me."

"There's just one other way we might find him," Jewle said. "And this is also between ourselves. We gathered he was very friendly with another of your employees—a woman named Wilson."

Painter smiled. "Look, Superintendent, what people do in their own time is no business of mine. I can assure you nothing ever took place here."

Jewle smiled too. "I'd be the last even to insinuate that there did. All I want to do is ask her about Dorne. Could you give me her address? I'm told she isn't here today."

Painter looked up from the drawer he'd opened. "Matter of fact she asked on Saturday if she might have three or four days off. Wasn't feeling too well. She might be along in the morning if you'd like to see her then."

"Think we'll go along now and get it over."

Painter gave the address: 73 Gordon Terrace, Camden Town.

Jewle thanked him, got to his feet and held out a hand. This time Painter even shook hands with me.

*

"No great hurry," Jewle said as we left Sandown Street. "Don't know about you but I'd like some lunch."

It suited me. It was well past my usual time. Jewle knew a little place in Soho. We had to wait five minutes for a seat but we got a meal in the end.

I asked what he'd thought of Painter.

"Beautifully veneered," he said. "A good-looker: nice smooth talker, and nicely muscled."

I couldn't help smiling. From what he'd said you'd have thought it an honour to be cracked on the skull by so charming a character.

"But you're not sure," he said. "When you last saw him that Saturday night he was at the counter."

I said that wasn't quite right. I'd seen him there during the evening but when I left I didn't look round at the counter. I just made my way through the tables, and the people, and out.

We finished the meal. Jewle paid and we made for Tottenham Court Road and took a bus. There's not much of London that Jewle doesn't know, and he soon had me lost once we'd got off. It took about five minutes to find Gordon Terrace, and a pretty drab-looking place it was. We knocked at the door of Number 73. A short-ish, plump-looking woman in the fifties opened it and I remember she was wiping her hands on her apron.

"Molly Wilson," Jewle said. "Doesn't she live here?"

"In the basement flat," she said. "You go down them steps, but she isn't there now. She's in hospital."

CHAPTER 10
THE SHOCK

SHE said we'd better come in. Were we relatives? Jewle said I was just an old friend. He just happened to be a police officer.

We stepped back forty years into the parlour. There were plush-seated chairs and a sofa to match. The round table had a fringed cloth and in the centre was a flattish bowl in which stood an aspidistra. The mantel-shelf was packed with ornaments and the fire in the grate beneath it showed a lonely spark of life. Three or four cheap prints hung from the picture rail and above the mantelpiece a slightly faded photograph of a soldier.

"You were saying she was in hospital," Jewle said. "What was the matter? Suddenly taken ill? What's your name, by the way?"

"Jarvis," she said. "Rose Jarvis. I'm a widow. My husband was killed in the last war."

"Right, Mrs. Jarvis. And now will you tell us what you know about Molly Wilson."

This was the story. She was glad of a bit of company and often used to pop down to Molly's place for a cup of tea and a chat. On the Monday morning she was going shopping and she noticed the milk hadn't been taken in and a newspaper was still poking through the letter-box. Molly had said nothing about going away, so she went down the steps to the door and listened. There were sounds like moans coming from inside so she tried the door. It was unlocked.

Molly was lying just inside the door of the bedroom and every now and again she was moaning. Mrs. Jarvis tried to lift her but she was too heavy and then she realised the best thing to do was to fetch the doctor. When the doctor came he sent for an ambulance and she was taken to St. Andrew's Hospital.

That was the gist of her story. Jewle asked no questions till it was over.

"Did the doctor tell you what was the matter with her?"

"No," she said, "but I could see for myself. She must have been out somewhere and fallen down the steps. Her face was all bruised. All night she must have been there. Trying to get to her bed; that's what she'd been doing."

"The bed hadn't been slept in?"

"No. It was just as she'd made it up the previous morning."

"Two pillows or one?"

Her face flushed slightly.

"I don't know nothing about that. It weren't no business of mine."

She'd still be there if we wanted her, so we got the doctor's address, thanked her and left.

"I don't like the look of it," Jewle said. "Mrs. Jarvis found her Monday morning and Dorne evidently didn't turn up the previous night. Probably he was killed on the Saturday night; in fact it's almost certain."

I said I didn't like that tale of a slip down the steps. There were only six of them. Jewle said he didn't like it either. Maybe the doctor could throw a little more light.

His name was Grasswood: house and surgery just two streets away from Gordon Terrace. We thought he'd be in and we were right. He looked a bit startled when Jewle's Warrant Card showed who we were. He said we'd better come in.

We went into his lounge. Jewle was perfectly frank. We'd called to see a patient of his—a Molly Wilson—hoping she might give us some information about a case we were on. The neighbour in the flat above had given us a rough idea of what had happened.

"That'd be Mrs. Jarvis," Grasswood said. "She was all out of breath when she got here and it took me a minute or two to find out what it was all about."

"And Molly Wilson? What was actually wrong with her?"

He was a youngish man—around thirty-five—and you could almost watch his brain pondering the implications of the Hippocratic oath.

"I have to know," Jewle said. "This is highly confidential but she'd got herself involved in a murder case. She didn't know it, but that's how it was. In any case what you tell us won't go any further. So just tell us what you know. The hospital can give us the rest."

"Very well then," he said. "I thought she'd had a very nasty fall somewhere and had tried to get to her bed and hadn't quite made it. She'd been lying there quite a time. I wanted her properly examined. And I foresaw a pneumonia danger."

"I understand from Mrs. Jarvis there were various bruises."

"Yes," he said. "One cheek was badly swollen and the left eye was virtually closed up."

"And you've had a report from the hospital?"

"Yes," he said. "I enquired this morning. She's on the danger list. Double pneumonia."

"Right," Jewle said and held out a hand. "Thanks for the information. I don't think we'll have to trouble you again."

"You're going to the hospital?"

"Yes. If she's said anything since admission, then we have to know what it was."

It turned out that he'd mentioned the hospital because it was a good quarter of an hour's walk away, and he was offering to take us in his car. We didn't hesitate about accepting. It was a pretty big place but he knew his way around. It was after he'd pointed out the enquiry desk that we thanked him again, and said goodbye. He looked just a bit disappointed as if he'd have liked to know a whole lot more.

The sister at Enquiries advised us to take a seat. It was the best part of five minutes later that the doctor who'd seen the patient on admission was ready.

"It's Doctor Lambert," she said. "He'll be waiting for you at the lift."

He was a man of around forty: quiet-looking and not at all impressed by Jewle's Warrant Card. We got out at the first floor. He said we could talk in his office.

Up to a certain point Jewle was frank.

"What you mean is that she's a witness?"

"More or less," Jewle said. "And now will you tell us what her injuries were exactly."

He smiled rather dryly and reeled off a list of contusions. He added, almost as an afterthought, a couple of broken ribs and a broken left wrist.

Jewle's smile was just as enigmatic. "And you're not going to tell me that that little list was the result of a fall?"

"Depends where she fell from and on what. All we know about that is what we heard from her doctor, and he had it at second-hand."

"Then I'll put you more in the picture," Jewle said. "No stairs in a basement flat. Only six steps down to the door from road level, and a rail to hold on by. Does that sound like a fall?"

"The way you put it, Superintendent—no. Unhappily she was in no condition to talk. Whether she ever will be is what concerns us at the moment. If she's still alive tomorrow and you'd like a man at her bedside, I'm sure we could provide facilities."

"Thanks," Jewle said. "And now a last question, Doctor. It's strictly confidential and I think you'll see its importance. Since the injuries scarcely seem the result of a fall, couldn't they more likely have been caused by what's known as a working-over?"

Lambert's lips tightened. He frowned. "Yes," he said slowly. "I think you might say that."

"Right," Jewle said. "Then we'll both forget the question was ever asked. I could see the patient?"

"I'd rather you didn't. It would serve no good purpose—unless you merely wanted to identify her."

"Oh, no," Jewle said. "My colleague here knows her very well. May I use your telephone?"

Lambert waved a hand. Jewle told him to stay put. In any case he couldn't have known what the call was all about. My guess was that he was asking about developments. Not much more than a minute and he was replacing the receiver.

"I needn't tell you, doctor, how grateful we are. I shouldn't have to trouble you or the hospital again, though I would like to be kept informed. Ask for me personally. The message will be taken if I'm not there."

Lambert told us the best way to the Yard: first to the right from the main entrance and a bus would take us almost anywhere. Less than five minutes' wait and one drew up that was going to Trafalgar Square. We went up to a sparsely occupied top.

There was nothing to argue about. Everything looked virtually cut and dried. Someone—probably the one who had searched Dorne's office—had had the idea that Molly Wilson might know where a missing something was, and he'd taken action accordingly. Whether or not he'd extracted the information he wanted, we didn't know. The odds were that he hadn't, and maybe because she'd none to give.

I asked if anything had happened at the Yard and all he would say was that enquiries in the docks' area were going on. He added that it wouldn't do any harm if both of us offered a prayer for the recovery of Molly Wilson. Just an answer by her to one simple question and the whole case would be cleared up.

We walked the short distance from Trafalgar Square, and it was after five o'clock when we got to the Yard. We were both a bit tired and Jewle had tea brought in. Another of his sergeants had some information. I was to ring Hallows at the agency.

Hallows told me how his enquiries had fared about Dorne, Ted Morris of United Enquiries had divulged that two years ago his agency had used Dorne and they'd afterwards proved to their own satisfaction that Dorne had double-crossed them with a client. Morris had taken confidential steps to have him black-listed.

"He said we must have been informed, too, and I said we hadn't. Then I checked with Norris and, sure enough, there it was."

I told him it didn't matter all that much. In any case it was Norris's own department. Jewle said it fitted in with what Painter had told us. From two years back Dorne had lost what had been a useful slice of income, which was why he'd been glad to do the em-cee-ing of Pop Nights twice a week.

Far more important was the finger-printing of Dorne's office. The smudges were just smudges, but from the pair of hand-grips at the desk front there'd been one or two clear prints. Jewle showed me the photographs.

"New to us," he said, "but probably a woman's. In the morning we'll check at the Wilson woman's flat."

There was nothing else for me. I'd told Hallows I'd be going straight home, and I did. In the morning I'd be seeing Jewle again at ten.

I wasn't used to walking long stretches on hard pavements and I felt pretty tired. After the evening meal I relaxed in an easy chair and looked up television programmes to take my mind completely off the case. There wasn't a thing that looked like doing it, so I looked through the programmes on radio. A really good concert would have been the ideal thing, but the only one was of modern music on the old Third Programme. Modern music's beyond me. The critics tell us we've only to school ourselves to listening and it will grow on us. To me that's the most arrogant form of humbug. I make no claims to musicianship but I've only to hear the opening bars of, say, a great symphony or concerto and, if the music then closed down, I could hum in my mind quite a deal of what was missed, and because it's become a pleasurable part of my musical memory. But I've painstakingly listened to quite a few modern symphonies and, if you were to offer me a thousand pounds a passage, I couldn't give you a couple of consecutive notes. To me they're just sounds: unrelated and generally discordant.

Mathis der Maler by Hindemith was the main work in that evening's concert and, as I said, it didn't appeal to me. Still the evening passed and, what was more, I had a good night's rest.

I'm almost sure it was my old friend La Rochefoucauld who remarked that no ignorance is half as dangerous as the knowledge of the partly informed. I'm no psychologist but I've always blandly assumed that when I wake in the morning with an answer to an overnight problem, it's because my subconscious has been delving down while the conscious slept and has come up with that answer.

Be that as it may, when I woke up in the morning, what I was saying to myself, and heaven knows why, was *Mathis der Maler*. Maler, I said: that's the German for painter.

Within a couple of minutes I was ringing Hallows. He's an earlier bird than I, and was having breakfast.

"Don't ask why," I said, "but put in a morning at Somerset House and also the immigration department of the Home Office and see if you can find any blood relationship between Geoff Marler and Martin Painter. See if Marler, the German refugee, changed his name at all on naturalisation. If you find anything out, give me a ring at the Yard."

He asked me to go over it again while he took it down.

"I've a vague idea I know some of the answers already," he told me. "It might be as well to check."

It was some time since I'd seen Marler but it wasn't hard to recall his face. The natty chin beard, of course, made him look older than he probably was. He was somewhat thinner than Painter but roughly the same height. Both were smooth talkers, but it was Marler who had the rough edges, and probably because his had been a different sort of life.

In any case, nothing was going to be said to Jewle till after Hallows' report: in fact, as soon as I picked up my morning paper, it went from my mind. Jewle, or his Higher-Ups, had decided on publicity, and the Dorne murder occupied the right-hand column of the front page, and that was publicity indeed for a paper so conservative as mine. There was even a photograph of Mayne House, that building in which Dorne had had his office.

Still, as far as I was concerned, what was most interesting was what was left out. Breakfast was ready and Bernice was calling, as wives have done since fire was first invented, that I was letting a hot meal get cold. As I sat down at the table I remembered something else. I think I clicked my tongue in annoyance.

"Something the matter?"

"Just something I ought to have remembered," I said "That Home and Family conference. Wasn't it yesterday?"

"I think so," she said. "I'm not sure."

"Could you find out? What about that friend of yours?"

I wasn't going to the agency unless Norris particularly wanted me. As it happened, he didn't. At half-past nine Bernice rang that friend of a friend. The conversation must have lasted two or three minutes.

"It *was* yesterday," I was told, "But Lady Marport wasn't there. She said it cast quite a damper on the proceedings."

"Did she say why she wasn't there?"

"A slight indisposition. Nothing, apparently, that a day or two in bed wouldn't cure. The meeting agreed unanimously to send good wishes for a quick recovery." She smiled. "I rather gathered it was like *Hamlet* without the prince."

She didn't ask any questions. Bernice is like that. When she lends a hand, she doesn't ask why.

As soon as I saw Jewle I told him about that absence. He listened but didn't seem to regard it as all that important. Maybe he had too much on his plate already. What ideas I had myself were entirely dependent on those theories we'd more or less vaguely formulated the day before: that Lady Marport had handed over money for her daughter's whereabouts and had been double-crossed. Absence from what should have been the great day of the year had been genuine enough. The shock or humiliation had genuinely upset her. Maybe, I thought, it mightn't be long before she was coming hat in hand to us.

I asked about Molly Wilson. Jewle said the news was much better. She was past the crisis and expected to make a good recovery. All the same it'd be at least a fortnight before she left that hospital.

The rest of his news was nearly all negative. Nothing from enquiries along the docks and nothing of great importance from Mayne House. Except one thing. A woman answering Molly's description had been seen there from time to time.

Apparently it was she who occasionally came early of a morning to give Dorne's place a bit of a clean.

"But not lately," Jewle said. "I think his business collapsed altogether the last few weeks, and he slept at her place. Maybe he turned up from time to time, just in case, but no more. He had the place on a seven-year lease and it's due for renewal at the end of the year, so he just didn't bother. If he paid his telephone bill, then he didn't trouble about its operating again."

"And Molly Wilson?" I said. "She can be questioned?"

"Not yet," he said. "The day after tomorrow, perhaps. Still, I managed to convince the hospital authorities and Downing's just gone along to take her prints. You know Downing?"

He meant Sergeant Downing of the Finger Print Department.

"We'd better get a move on," he said. "He's to go to Gordon Terrace straight from the hospital. We're supposed to be meeting him there."

This time we went by car. When we got to Number 73 we found the door of the basement flat locked.

"You stay here," Jewle told me. "I'll have a word with Mrs. Jarvis."

Before he was back Downing's car drew in. He's on the short side and sturdy. Practically all his life he has been in the Print Department but you'd still take him for a farmer. He can cast an apparently casual eye over a print and identify it at once. I've swatted the whole thing up but to me ridge characteristics are still almost hieroglyphics.

He said he had a lovely set of Wilson prints and, while we were talking, Jewle came back, and Rose Jarvis was with him. She hadn't liked the thought of the flat door open all night, so she'd gone to the agent who handled rents and got a spare key.

Jewle must have done a lot of explaining. As soon as we were inside, Downing took her prints. Jewle thanked her and she left. Downing, metaphorically pawing the ground, got to work. Jewle and I had a general look round.

It was a smallish flat: living-room, bedroom, small bathroom-lavatory and a compact kitchen with cupboards for pantry and an electric stove. The made-up bed did have two pillows.

Rose Jarvis may have thought the place was just a bit disorderly: to us it was clear that the whole flat had been searched. It wasn't anything like a shambles. Whoever had done the searching had taken pains to put everything back in something resembling order. Even the bed had been clumsily re-made and the pillows nicely smoothed.

Downing called to us from the kitchen. He'd been there about twenty minutes.

"Wilson prints all over the place," he said, "and a couple of Dorne's."

"They tally?"

"Of course they tally. Whose else did you expect to find?"

"Look," Jewle said patiently. "I know they tally. But do the Wilson prints tally with those from Mayne House?"

"Oh, them," Downing said. "Nothing like it. I'd say the Mayne House prints were left by a much younger woman. Clearer—what there are of 'em."

"You're sure?"

"Of course I'm sure."

Jewle looked flabbergasted.

"Incredible! I'd have bet a week's pay it was Wilson who was in Dorne's office. It had to be her. It couldn't be anyone else."

"Well, it was," Downing said. "I'll keep on trying if you like."

"You do that," Jewle said. "We'll have a cup of coffee. There's a place not far back."

There was a Lyons' in the High Street. We had coffee and a cake and most of the time Jewle was on edge. I didn't remember seeing him like that before. It was a mystery to me too, though I wasn't all that involved. It could only have been Dorne who had hidden that something in his office, and Molly Wilson should have been the only possible one he had sent to reclaim it.

Just as we were leaving, Jewle had an idea. "Wait a minute. She couldn't have known of Dorne's death."

"That's right," I said. "But what difference does it make?" He shook his head. "Don't know. It was just an idea." When we got back Downing was standing by our car. He said he'd finished and had taken back the key. There was no need to ask any questions. It was definitely not Molly Wilson who had left those prints in Mayne House.

CHAPTER 11
THE FIRST BREAK

IT WAS well after midday when we got back to the Yard. I took a chance and rang Hallows. He was not only in: he was bursting with information. He said things had been easier because of that earlier enquiry into Geoff Marler. It was easier, too, for me to follow. Jewle was a different proposition. He'd seen only an incomplete version in the Marport file, so I drew him a family tree.

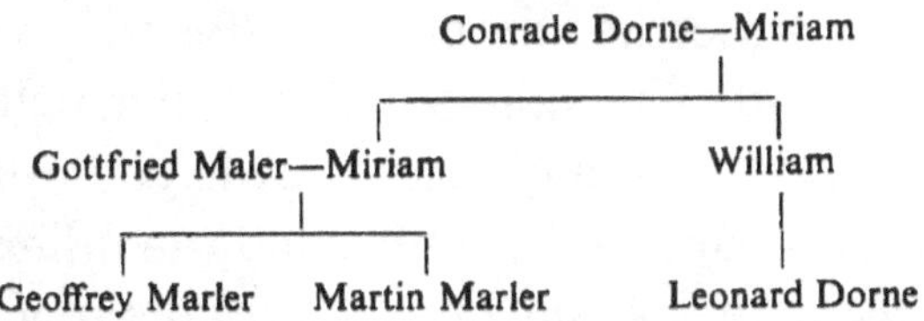

Conrade Dorne, I repeated, was the founder of the photographic business and his wife was Jewish. They had a daughter named Miriam and a son, William. The daughter married a German named Maler, and when hostility against the Jews started to become open, they came to England. When Maler was naturalised, he changed his name to Marler. Meanwhile the son, William, had married and he had just the one son—Leonard Dorne. The Marlers had two sons. The younger—our Martin Painter—later changed the name. Maybe he didn't like his own name—Marler. The two sons had probably been brought up to be bilingual, so he'd know the original family name, Maler, was German for the English Painter.

"So those two are brothers," Jewle said. "And Dorne was their first cousin. How'd you get on to it?"

Just a memory, I said, of the German I'd learned at school and since largely forgotten. I added that it made sense that one of Marler's models should come from Painter's place. Maybe the other one—the one we'd followed to Holloway, had taken a course there too.

Jewle said he'd never had even a suspicion of the relationships: different names, and businesses a good half-mile apart.

"Don't let's jump too far ahead," he said. "What you've found out alters things: make no mistake about that, but let's keep building on supposition. Let's say all three were in some swindle or other. Money was received, almost certainly by Dorne, then the other two found he was about to operate another swindle of his own, like bolting with the proceeds, and in a quarrel, Dorne got knifed. One of the others searched his office and the other beat up Molly Wilson, in case she knew where the money was."

"It fits in," I said, "but there's something it doesn't explain—that thing the size of an envelope that was cellophaned under Dorne's table. And who the woman was who probably took it away. That makes four to consider, not three."

He thought for a moment, then got to his feet. "Let's go and see Marler. We'll take a chance on his not having gone to lunch."

Downstairs I went on ahead. Before he rejoined me, I saw him having a word with the driver of another car. It moved round and ahead of us and was gone by the time we'd moved off too.

"What was all that?"

"Something just in case," he said. "Depends on whether or not Marler's in."

He was driving, so I didn't ask any more questions. It wasn't far to Marler's place and we were lucky with traffic lights. There was just room for the car to back into an open place.

"You go ahead," he said. "They know you. If he's in, I'll do the talking."

The secretary was in her office. I rapped at the door and went in. Jewle was at my elbow. She gave a slight smile as she recognised me.

"Good-morning," I said. "Mr. Marler in?"

"I'm almost sure he's in his office."

"Then don't bother," I said. "We'll go right through. He's probably expecting us."

Marler was at his desk. He looked slightly startled at the sudden sight of me.

"Hope we're not disturbing you, Mr. Marler. This is Chief-Superintendent Jewle of New Scotland Yard."

There was a moment's hesitation before he took Jewle's outstretched hand.

"You've seen this morning's paper?" Jewle said.

"Yes," Marler said. "I suppose you mean about Len Dorne." He shook a sorrowful head. "A horrible business, sir. Horrible."

"It is indeed. That's why we rather expected you to ring us."

"Me!" He stared. "Why should I do that, sir?"

"You're his first cousin," Jewle said. "Surely there was something you could have told us? Or wanted to ask us?"

"No, sir; you're wrong there. I only saw him once in a blue moon, as they say. It isn't as if he was a close relation: I mean a brother, or anything like that."

"You knew he worked regularly for your brother?"

There was a slight hesitation. "I suppose I did. To tell the truth, sir, I didn't know much about it. It isn't all that often I see my brother."

Jewle stopped sparring. "Right, Mr. Marler. Now there's something I have to ask you to do. We want a further identification of that cousin of yours for the purposes of the inquest." He cut short the expostulation. "Sorry, but I have to insist. It won't take all that long. My car's outside."

Marler put on his overcoat and hat. Jewle ushered him out and we went straight through to the car. I opened the rear door for Marler and got in beside him.

It took a good twenty minutes to get to that dockside mortuary. I didn't do any prattling: just an occasional word. Jewle, I imagined, would want him to stew in his own juice. When our car drew in, another car was already there: the one that had gone ahead of us at the Yard.

Marler seemed to like mortuaries as little as I did. He looked nervously about him and gave a little shiver as we went in. I watched him as the attendant pulled out the tray. Jewle beckoned him forward and drew back the sheet.

"You recognise him?"

Marler had to clear his throat before he could speak. "Yes, sir. It's him."

"That's capital. Just what we needed. By the way, he was stabbed in the back, most likely with a flick-knife. You probably read about that too. You'd like to see the wound?"

He made as if to draw the sheet back.

"No," he said, "No!"

"That's all right." Jewle drew the sheet on again. "Not a very pleasant sight. We're pretty hardened to it ourselves."

He nodded to the attendant and I thought for a moment he was going to take Marler's arm.

"That's all, Mr. Marler. We're very grateful for your assistance. My driver will take you back."

He moved off with Marler to that other car but we managed to get away first. Jewle chuckled.

"Just a little stratagem. The driver's been told to keep moving but make it steady. We don't want Marler getting in touch with his brother. It's his place we're off to now."

I was itching to ask his impressions of Marler, but driving was tricky and I said hardly a word till at last we drew into Sandown Street.

"There's a resemblance to his brother," he said, "but I can't say I liked that fancy beard." He pulled himself together as if he'd been wool-gathering. "You mean his reactions? What'd you think yourself?"

"I wouldn't call him scared but he was very, very careful, if you know what I mean. And he really had to pull himself together in the mortuary."

He backed the car in. "Right," he said. "Let's have a word with our friend Painter."

The same secretary-receptionist was at the desk. I think she was having a scratch lunch—sandwiches from the coffee bar?—for she hastily covered something up with a folder at the sight of us, but there were bread-crumbs on the table.

"I see you remember us," Jewle said. "Mr. Painter in?"

"I'm afraid not, sir. He went to lunch about twenty minutes ago."

"You know where?"

"Well, it might be the Silver Spoon. He generally goes there."

"Just off Shaftesbury Avenue?"

She flushed slightly. "I think it is."

Jewle smiled. "Mind if I ask your name?"

"Brooks. Tessa Brooks."

"Then thank you, Miss Brooks. When Mr. Painter comes in you might tell him we called. Nothing urgent. By the way, I see you read the *Daily Picture*. You've read about your Mr. Dorne?"

"Yes," she said. "It's terrible. It's upset everyone."

"I'm sure it has." He smiled down again. "Well, we've got to be going. Thank you again."

He didn't move the car on at once. He asked me what I thought of Miss Brooks.

"A very pretty woman," I said. "Nice figure too."

"She's all that," he said, and smiled. "Like to hear a bit of fanciful deduction?"

I laughed. "Go ahead."

"I think she and Painter are on very good terms. Notice that blush when she mentioned the Silver Spoon? Painter's probably taken her there."

He moved the car on without waiting for comment. When we turned off Shaftesbury Avenue it took another five minutes to find a parking place.

From the outside the Silver Spoon looked a pretty expensive place. From the handsome vestibule just beyond the bar, we looked through the glass door into the almost full restaurant. Painter was lunching alone at a table in the far corner.

"You're not taking him anywhere? The mortuary, for instance?"

"No, no," he said. "Just a little friendly chat."

"Then I'll stand you a lunch," I said.

He demurred, then gave in. It was almost two o'clock and I was uncommonly hungry. We deposited hats and overcoats and the head waiter showed us to a table. Jewle took out his wallet.

"That man in the far corner, there. As soon as he gets up to go—"

"You mean Mr. Painter, sir?"

"Yes. Soon as he gets up to go, call his attention to us and say we'd like to see him."

A note changed hands. We took our seats and had a look at the menu. With a weather eye open for Painter, the head waiter himself took our orders. Too many tables lay between us and Painter for us to be seen.

"Seems as if they know him here," I said.

He grunted. "Lucky for him. Wouldn't mind having a few meals here myself."

It was cold outside. The soup was hot and it was good. I was just finishing mine when I caught sight of Painter and the head waiter threading a way towards us. Jewle got to his feet. Painter looked rather amused.

"Didn't expect to see you here, Superintendent?" He turned the look on me. "And how are you sir?"

"Bearing up," I said. "Shan't keep you more than a minute."

Another chair was found. Painter sat down. The fawn, Carnaby Street coat somehow accentuated the broad shoulders.

"You've read about Dorne?" Jewle said. "If so, we think you might have got in touch with us."

"In touch? Why?"

"Dammit," Jewle said, "you employed him. He was your cousin. Didn't his murder mean anything to you?"

"Of course it did. It was a pretty horrible thing to happen. All the same, he had his own private life. And what's a cousin? It wasn't as if he was a close relative or anything like that." He shook his head. "Len wasn't anything to me—not really. Just someone I employed. Besides—"

He hesitated.

"Besides what?"

Painter shrugged his shoulders. "Well, I know it may sound callous but I didn't want any publicity. It wouldn't do my place any good."

"I get your point," Jewle said. "When did you see him last?"

"But I told you. Saturday."

"But he couldn't have turned up last Wednesday. What about that?"

Painter shrugged his shoulders again. "He was like that. Now and again he didn't turn up. We managed. I thought perhaps he'd got himself a client."

"And Molly Wilson. Has she turned up?"

He looked surprised.

"Matter of fact, she hasn't. I sent someone round yesterday afternoon and the place was locked. You know something about her?"

"Yes," Jewle said. "She's in hospital. It'll be two or three days before she can be seen, so don't bother to take any flowers."

"I can't believe it. What's wrong with her?"

"Had a nasty fall," Jewle said. "That's the official belief. Strictly between ourselves, I think someone gave her a going-over."

"My God, no!" He drew himself up with a quick indignation. "Who the hell would do a thing like that? Molly wouldn't have hurt a fly."

"Maybe it was someone who thought she knew something about Dorne. Wanted to keep her mouth shut. You can't throw any light on it yourself?"

His eyes narrowed. "Look here, Superintendent, you're not insinuating—"

"Insinuating nothing," Jewle said mildly. "No need to fly off the handle. Just a simple question. And, after all, she *was* pretty friendly with Dorne." He got to his feet and I followed suit. "Sorry we kept you. You'll want to be getting back to Sandown Street."

"You're right," he said. "Still, anything I can do to help, if you know what I mean."

He made none too graceful an exit. Jewle let out a breath. I signalled to the waiter. A minute or two and he was bringing the second course.

"God, how I hate that fellow!" Jewle said. "Did you notice anything queer about anything he said?"

"Only something that looked like collusion. He and Marler said practically the same thing—that bit about what's a cousin and not like a brother."

"You're right," he said. "Those two put their heads together. That's the galling part. There's nothing we can do about it—not yet."

I asked him what he actually knew about Painter. He said he now knew quite a lot. In his teens he'd done a lot of amateur boxing with a Shoreditch club and later he'd turned pro.

"That's another queer thing," he said. "He never was more than a second or third rater so where did he get the money to open a gym? That was at Tottenham in partnership with a character called Harpenden. We got him a year or two later for touting pep pills. Couldn't pin anything on Painter. He opened a club, still in Totten-ham, and ran it up to a couple of years ago when he got the lease on his present place. We had a tip-off about pep pills but couldn't get any evidence."

He gave his dry smile. "Queen Mary had *Calais* written on her heart. Know what'll be written on mine? *Where did Painter get the money from?*"

We didn't stay on for coffee. As it was, we were almost the last ones in the restaurant. He rang the Yard from there but there was nothing new.

He drove me to Broad Street, and the way we left things was that he'd ring me in the morning if there looked like being anything I could do.

"I'm going to that hospital," he said. "Painter will probably find out which one it is and I don't want him to do any personal calling."

I didn't hear from him till the following afternoon. He said he was seeing Molly Wilson in the morning. If I'd like to go along, he'd pick me up at the flat at about ten.

In a minute or two Bertha would be bringing in a cup of tea. The continuity of what I'd been doing had been broken by Jewle's call, so I took a breather. Even before I had my pipe going I was thinking about Molly Wilson and what Jewle had suggested to Painter in the Silver Spoon. I wondered if Painter had kept to himself the news about her, or if he'd said something to his staff. There was an easy way to find out: just ring Tessa Brooks.

I was just about to call Bertha when something came back—what Jewle had thought was a possible relationship between Painter and his receptionist. Another minute and I was in Bertha's little office. She said she was just about to take in my tea.

"I'll have it here," I said. "There's something I want you to do. First I'll put you in the picture and then we'll write the script."

The only person I'd met at Painter's place, or connected with it, was Susan Farley. Hers, at least, was the only name. The fact that I had every reason to distrust her now seemed to make little difference, since all I wanted was for news of Molly Wilson to get to the staff. Someone might remember something and even be prepared to tell.

It took us a quarter of an hour to write and rehearse that script. Bertha dialled the number. I was listening in.

"Sorry to disturb you but could I speak to Miss Farley?"

"Who's speaking, please?"

"Mrs. Porter. It's rather urgent."

"I think she should be finishing a class, Mrs. Porter. If she's free I'll put you through."

(So far so good. In exactly one minute the line was open again.)

"Yes? This is Susan Farley."

"Oh, Miss Farley, I'm Mrs. Porter. Vera Porter. Are you a friend of Molly Wilson? I'm sure I once heard her mention you."

(There was a short silence. Call it a hesitation.)

"Well, you could call me that. Everyone here knew Molly. Why do you ask?"

"Well, I went to see her this morning and she wasn't in and then a neighbour of hers told me she was in St. Andrew's Hospital, and how the police had been making enquiries."

"The police?"

"Yes. From Scotland Yard. According to the neighbour, she'd been attacked in the flat and ever so badly hurt. Have you heard anything yourself? The hospital wouldn't tell me anything except she'd been on the danger list and no one could see her."

"But how dreadful! It's the first we've heard of anything here. We all thought she'd gone away for a short holiday."

"Well, I thought I'd better let someone know. It won't be any use trying to see her, though, not for three or four days. If I do hear anything else, would you like me to let you know?"

"I would, please. In the afternoon. I might be away in the morning."

That was all, except for the goodbyes. That was fine, I told Bertha. Couldn't have gone off better.

Those weren't just words. I was really pleased. In a very short time the whole of Painter's staff would have the news. Maybe it would get round to the patrons. One other thing it would do was to present Painter himself with a problem, especially the news that Scotland Yard was working on the supposition that Molly had been attacked.

And, when I got to thinking of it, it looked as if Painter had said nothing to his staff, unless it was that Molly was away on that holiday. It was pretty certain too that he'd kept to himself the fact that she was in hospital.

The next morning I didn't go down to wait for Jewle. He and Bernice are old friends and I guessed he'd come up to the flat. He did, and he brought the Marport file with him. Bernice wanted to make coffee but he said he was a bit late.

The car had hardly moved off when he was telling me something.

"I meant to have told you this when I rang you yesterday afternoon, but someone—a woman—rang us and said she was a friend of Molly Wilson. To cut it short, she wanted to know if we could tell her what hospital she was in. We didn't take the call ourselves but I went into it and the voice might have been that of our friend Tessa Brooks. I said *might*."

"Painter finding out where Molly Wilson was?"

"Could have been," he said. "And one other thing. I took that Doctor Lambert further into my confidence and last night Molly Wilson was told that Dorne was dead. He said she took it almost as if she'd known it was going to happen, but when the sister saw her a few minutes later, she'd been crying.

"What I wanted," he went on, "was for all that to be over before she was questioned this morning. The last thing wanted was hysteria. Also she'd have a night's sleep and be able to think things over."

I said he couldn't have done better.

"You're pinning a lot of hopes on this interview, aren't you?"

He gave a dour shake of the head. "You bet I am."

That was all he said. Traffic was pretty dense and I asked no more questions. Also I wanted to do some thinking for myself.

CHAPTER 12
DISCOVERY

WE HAD to wait a short time in Lambert's office before he could join us. When he did, you couldn't tell from his expression if his news was going to be good or bad.

"How is she?" Jewle said.

Lambert pursed his lips.

"In herself? Getting on quite well. All the same, I think you're going to have a tough time."

"Why?"

"Well, we couldn't spring you people on her. She had to be told a police officer was coming to ask her one or two questions. She took it so badly I didn't pursue it."

"What's badly?"

"Well, to put it bluntly, she saw no reason to be questioned by the police. All she'd had was a fall."

He looked at his watch. Everything was ready. But no persistent questioning. Five minutes at the very most and as quiet as Jewle could make it. There was a last word at the door. At the least sign of hysteria, the bedside bell was to be pushed. He wagged a final finger.

"Five minutes. Less if you can make it but not a second more."

The almost bare room had just the one bed. Between it and the usual bedside table was a cane-bottomed chair. Another chair was on the far side. A chart hung on the bed-rail and there was a faintly hissing sound from an air-locked radiator by the far wall. When I look back now, what I chiefly remember is the pale face on the pillow and eyes that looked enormously dark. As I neared I could see a thin plaster strip above an eye. A bruise on the cheek was a yellowish-green.

If I'd not known who she was, I'd never have taken her for Molly Wilson. Molly had been registered in my memory as a tallish, buxom woman laughing at some joke she was sharing with Bob Hallows. Lambert began talking as he, too, neared the bed. Brutus called it smiles and affability: we call it a good bedside manner. He was definitely smiling as he looked down.

"Still feeling better, are we?" He waved a hand. "These are the two gentlemen I was telling you about. They don't look like anything to be afraid of; now do they? So you just answer the questions and then sister will be in with your milk."

He gave us a nod as he virtually tiptoed out. Jewle turned the chair to face the head that was almost sideways on the pillow. He sat quietly down and the room had a queer sort of silence till he began to speak.

"We are very glad to hear you were getting better, Miss Wilson. You must have had a terrible time. You're sure you're feeling well enough to answer one or two simple questions?"

The lips moved. She must have said yes.

"Then just tell me who it was that beat you up that night in your flat. Who it was that nearly killed you?"

"Nobody did," she said, and the unexpected vigour of the voice almost startled me. "It wasn't that at all. I just tripped over something and fell on my face down the steps."

"Oh, no," Jewle said. "We know better. I can't tell you how we know, but we definitely know. Doctor Lambert knows. Everyone here knows, so why should you go on trying to protect someone who might have killed you?"

"I'm not," she said. "You're all wrong. There wasn't anybody. I just fell."

Jewle went quietly on. "If you're afraid of him, you needn't be. From now on you'll be protected. So who was he, Miss Wilson? Just tell me his name. Nothing else: just his name."

She shook her head. He waited a moment.

"You liked Leonard Dorne? He'd never have beaten you up. You and he had some good times together. No more good times, though. The same one who beat you up murdered him. That's why we want his name. Do you want him to go free?" She shook her head again. Maybe she was going to talk after all. Then the lips began to pucker and she was crying. The quiet sobbing could just be heard against that soft hissing of the radiator.

Jewle got quietly to his feet. He watched impassively till the sobbing had ceased.

"That's better," he said. "Sometimes there's nothing else for it but to have a nice, quiet cry. Here, take my handkerchief."

She dabbed at her eyes. He waited till she'd finished and slowly eased the handkerchief from her fingers.

"Think just once more," he said. "You've only got to tell me one name and then we'll leave you to yourself. Who was the man? Don't say it. Just whisper it. Something strictly between you and me."

He bent right down. Her eyes were closed and the lips were obstinately still. The room had suddenly a different kind of quiet. It had an eerie sort of tension.

Then Jewle slowly straightened himself and at the same time there was a warning tap at the door. Lambert's finger was beckoning and we went quietly out.

"And how did it go?" Lambert said.

"Hopeless. There was just one moment when I thought something was coming—but no. Maybe I didn't handle her the right way."

"Rubbish!" I said. "No one could have handled her better. There wasn't an angle you didn't try."

We went back to Lambert's office. Jewle didn't seem too keen, but I accepted the offer of a cup of coffee. It had been a heartbreaking morning for Jewle.

"Why didn't she talk?" he asked us. "All she had to do was whisper just one name. Who's she protecting? Not herself. She'd have spoken if it'd been just that."

"Perhaps she's thinking well ahead," I said. "Sooner or later she'll be leaving here, which means, to her, that she'll be alone again in that flat."

"May I make a suggestion?" That was Lambert. "If you had someone outside her door from now on, wouldn't that give her confidence? It wouldn't inconvenience us to have a man stationed outside—"

He broke off.

"Good heavens!" He chuckled. "That was lucky. Something I ought to've remembered. I shan't be a minute."

"What was all that?" Jewle said. He closed the door Lambert had left open. "One minute he'd making suggestions and then he's off like a bat out of hell."

"Maybe he remembered where he left the scalpel."

Jewle wasn't amused. In any case he didn't have long to find out. Lambert came back, all smiles. In his hand was what looked like a rumpled sheet of blueish paper.

"It was that word *station*," he said. "I knew there was something I wanted you to see."

Jewle looked at it. His eyes bulged a little.

"Where'd you get this?"

"I only knew about it yesterday. When she was being prepared for bed the nurse found it. It must have been under her foot inside the stocking. Nurse mentioned it to the sister and yesterday sister mentioned it to me."

I'd had a look at it too. It was a receipt from a left-luggage office.

"I'll have to take this," Jewle said. "I'll give you a receipt. That be all right?"

He wrote it at Lambert's desk, and thought it was well if I signed it too. You couldn't quite call the haste indecent, but he didn't waste much time over goodbyes. In the car he did wait a minute before moving off. It was the thrill of what might be the big break. He had to get the feeling of it out of his system.

"That's why she clammed up," he told me. "She was waiting till she got out and could get whatever it is out of that left-luggage office."

He gave himself a little nod of approval and moved the car on. We didn't drive fast and it was a good twenty minutes later when we drew in at the fore-court of Charing Cross Station. "You stay here," he told me. "I'll do the collecting."

He was back in a couple of minutes and what he had with him was a battered-looking brief-case: leather tarnished strap handles well worn and a film of rust on the metal-work. Whatever was in it was bulky but yielding, like wadded paper.

"It's locked," he told me.

I began feeling for my pen-knife.

"No," he said. "We'd better leave it intact."

We moved out into the traffic, waited a minute at the lights and on to the Yard.

"You go up," he said. "Be with you in a couple of minutes."

He was longer than that, but there was a key in the lock of that case when he came in. He was still optimistic judging by his smile.

"Never accuse me of lacking in self-restraint," he said. "Thought we'd look inside together."

We were right about the wadded paper. At the very bottom was something else. I knew from the look on his face that he'd struck rich. His hand came out with two or three bundles of notes. It went in again, rummaged around and came out with one or two more. He upended the case and shook it.

"That's the lot."

He counted. He flicked one of the packets.

"That's it," he said. "Six packets of a hundred used five-pound notes. If my arithmetic's right, that's exactly three thousand pounds." He frowned. "Somehow five thousand would have made more sense."

He explained. It looked as if those tenuous theories of ours had had the very devil of a lot of substance. Painter and Dorne, and perhaps Marler. Somehow they'd operated a pretty paying scheme. Dorne had been the one to collect the cash.

"Somehow three thousand doesn't fit in," he said. "It doesn't sound right. Five thousand, ten thousand—that'd have been better."

He said we'd leave that part of it. What didn't need explaining was that Dorne himself hadn't been entitled to at least the whole of that money.

"We were right then," I said. "He was double-crossing the others and doing a bolt."

"Not just that," he said. "The way I begin to see it is that he had the money but he must have had an appointment with Painter to hand it over and then take his share. What I think he did was deposit the money, give the receipt to Molly Wilson for safe keeping and then have a prepared yarn to tell Painter. The money hadn't been ready, for instance: anything to make time. Painter didn't believe it and that was that."

"And Painter guessed it had to be Molly who had the money." I think I winced. "She must have been a damn plucky woman to keep her mouth shut, and all the time that receipt hidden under her foot."

"Yes," he said. "Keeping her mouth shut with me this morning was nothing compared with that."

We got down to the real question of where that money had come from. Had the whole thing centred round the missing Beryl Marport? Whether it had or not, it was the only supposition to explore.

"Lady Marport's private account. Surely you could get the bank manager to say if he'd prepared and handed over a large amount in used five-pound notes? That would also tell us if it was more than this three thousand."

He shook a slow head.

"It's not all that easy. We can't go that far on a mere theory. She's apparently a pretty important woman. If any of what we suspect is wrong, I'll be on a spot. What I'll do is give it a lot of thought over the week-end. I'll almost certainly have to put it up to the Commander."

So that, as they say, was that. I signed a formal statement about the case and its contents, and a minute or two later I left. I also had in front of me a week-end in which to think.

Late autumn and early winter had been the worst I'd ever known: rain and wind and only a day or so's respite and then more rain and wind, and most of it most damnably cold. That Saturday hadn't been at all bad and, when I took a look out on the Sunday morning, I could hardly credit what I saw. The sun was actually shining and, when I switched on the radio, the weather report said we were in for at least twenty-four hours of warmer weather, with only the possibility of an occasional shower.

Just after breakfast the telephone went. I guessed it was Jewle, but I was wrong. It was Laurie Steevens.

"It's about that job Daddy said I'd do for you," she said. "Sorry I couldn't ring you last night."

"No hurry," I said. "You mean the job about our missing friend?"

"Yes," she said. "I did some talking at that Old Girls' do, and all I could get was David Prentiss. That's spelt with a double-ess. He and Beryl were apparently rather friendly, so he might know where she is. I think it's a pretty long shot myself."

I said it was worth a try. Did she have his address?

"It's a village named Little Warfield. Near Saffron Walden. I don't know the name of the house but his people are lords of the manor or squires or something, so anyone's bound to know."

I said I was most grateful. A few pleasant words and we were ringing off.

Sunday morning means a dressing-gown breakfast at half-past eight and then settling comfortably down to a pipe and a paper. I suppose I was a bit restless that morning. Speaking with Laurie Steevens had brought my mind back to the Marport case, and somehow I couldn't settle down. It was through thinking of Laurie again that I had a sudden idea. Far too rare a day to stay indoors, I told Bernice, so what about a ride in the country?

It's not too easy to pull wool over her eyes so I said frankly that I'd have to make a country trip the next day, when the weather mightn't be half as good, so why not go when the going was good? She thought it a great idea, so I rang a hotel I knew and booked lunch. It was just after ten when we set off.

There wasn't too much traffic on the roads. In any case we were in no hurry, and it was just short of eleven when I pulled up at the cross-roads. To the right was Saffron Walden: Little Warfield was five miles to the left.

East of Saffron Walden is my native country. Little Warfield, to the west, I'd never seen before. It was a scattered, unpretentious sort of place: small copses here and there and narrowish, twisty roads. There was a minute green with an embroidery of cottages and the tower of the church was just visible among the elms.

There wasn't a soul in sight so I stopped at a cottage and asked for the Prentiss place. It was in a side road and not hard to find. The late Georgian house was like a country vicarage but far better kept. The gravel drive had few weeds: ornamental hedges had been clipped and a few late roses were still on the climber that ran along the south wall and over the porch.

I drew the car in where a narrowish opening between some bushes led back along the side of the house. There had been a queer noise and I'd wondered what it could be. I got out to investigate, and as soon as I was in the open I knew exactly what it was. I went on a few yards and was facing a kind of yard by some outhouses. A young man in a turtle-necked sweater, slacks and gum-boots was hosing down a small sports car. He should never have been allowed to sing.

I had a good look at him and somehow I liked what I saw. The blond hair was neatly cut, not long, and he had an attractive, somewhat humorous face. His height was about five-ten and his age around twenty.

He caught sight of me as I moved forward. The singing stopped and he gave me a somewhat quizzical look.

"David Prentiss?"

"Yes," he said.

"My name's Travers. I'm a friend of Laurie Steevens and Beryl Marport."

He smiled. "Ah, Beryl. How is she?"

"Look," I said. "I want to talk with you seriously. Something rather unfortunate's happened and perhaps you might help us."

I explained the *us* by saying my wife was in the car.

"We'd better go in the house," he said. "I'll get these damn gum-boots off. You mean that something's happened to Beryl?"

He took the boots off in the garage and put on some slippers. He gave me a friendly grin.

"My people are at church so I'm on my own, so to speak."

The slippers meant careful going. We made it to the car. I did the introductions: said Mr. Prentiss and I were going to have a short talk in the house.

"Can't Mrs. Travers come too, sir? I'll get Emma to make us all some coffee."

Five minutes later we were in the cheerful warmth of a lounge, sipping at scalding hot coffee. I began telling him about Beryl. He winced slightly at the mention of Lady Marport's name.

"I'm not surprised," he said. "She was always pretty independent. Knew her way around."

"You first met her at those school dances?" I said. "You young fellows must have found them very enjoyable."

He smiled. "Indeed we did. There was an awful lot of competition to get invited. It was great fun."

"What sort of dancing?" Bernice said. "Pop dancing, if that's the right word?"

He laughed. "Lord, no! Far more decorous. Back to Victoria, if you know what I mean. Good fun, though. To tell the truth, the girls there were pretty good. It took some getting used to for us."

"When was the last time you saw Beryl?"

"Easter week. I think it was the Wednesday. We went to an Italian film and then had tea. I'd suggested lunch but she already had a date."

"You don't know with whom? Pardon my being persistent but her mother's very worried, as you can guess."

"Of course, sir." He frowned. "Let me see now. I was to meet her outside a restaurant called the Silver Spoon just before two o'clock—"

"Isn't that just off Shaftesbury Avenue?"

"That's right," he said. "About a hundred yards away. So I hung around and just before two she came out with a man. A smooth-looking gent in a natty overcoat. I remember I rather quizzed her about him."

"I think I know who he was."

I gave a description of Painter. He said I was right. That was definitely the man.

"Did she tell you anything about him herself?"

"I forget," he said. "I think she just explained him away as a family friend."

"And that was the very last time you saw her?"

"Yes," he said. "The very last time."

I showed him that head and shoulders photograph. He gave a sort of approbatory smile.

"That's frightfully good of her. Did you take it, sir?"

"Afraid not," I said. "Borrowed it, as a matter of fact." I passed it to Bernice. "What you'd call a clever face, I think."

"She looks charming," she said. "Must have been a delightful dancing partner."

"She was," he said. He frowned slightly. "A pity I rather lost sight of her. There weren't any dances in their summer term. Only occasional tennis. Hardly my line."

Time was running on. At any moment his people might be back from church, so I said we had to be going. He went with us to the car.

"Sorry I couldn't be of more help."

I said we'd just have to go on looking. But he could do me one more favour. If by any chance he had any news of her would he give me a ring.

There was room to circle the car round. He waved another farewell as we passed.

"What a charming boy!" Bernice said. "And so nicely mannered."

I threw just a little more light on the disappearance of Beryl Marport. She was entitled to that. I wasn't surprised that the little she said had quite a Beryl bias.

We drove another ten miles to a good lunch. We made a leisured and circuitous way home and by then it was time for tea and, as I lighted my pipe and settled in my chair, I told myself it'd been a curious sort of day. Strangely enough I found it hard to assess just what had been the real value of what I'd learned.

Even when I did make what seemed at the moment a fairly satisfying assessment, I was to be utterly wrong. It wasn't what I might call the hard news that was really to matter, but the apparent trivialities.

CHAPTER 13
FANTASTIC DAY

THE next morning I was at the Yard at about half-past ten. Jewle hadn't rung me but I had things he ought to be glad to hear. I rapped at the door and looked in. Sergeant Harries was there, and he seemed to be merely waiting. He said Jewle had been in conference for best part of an hour so he ought to be in at any moment. He offered me a cigarette and I politely accepted.

The only news he could give was negative. The ash of the cigarette was getting ominously long so I went across to Jewle's desk for an ash-tray. The only official looking paper on it was a sheet with a couple of rows of figures.

"What's all this?" I said.

He came across.

"You remember, sir, the telephone numbers Dorne had noted on the wall? That's what they are. We copied them down and I've been trying to trace."

"Any luck?"

"None," he said. "If you look at them you'll see only five of the twenty or so have anything but the actual number. No exchange."

I frowned for a moment. "That makes sense. Once you've rung a number you'd remember the exchange. It's the number itself you'd be likely to forget. Or am I wrong?"

"I expect you're right, sir. All I know is there wasn't anything to be got from those I called. At least anything to do with what we're on."

I had a look at them. A moment or two and I stopped, as it were, in mid-air. I took out my notebook.

"Found something, sir?"

"Yes," I said. "Don't look surprised if you should be told about it but—"

I broke off. Jewle was just coining in.

"Been waiting long?" he said.

"Only a few minutes. Good job I did. Harries and I have just made a discovery. This list of telephone numbers from Dorne's office. One of them is Lady Marport's private address."

He stared. "You're sure?"

I showed him the entry in my notebook.

"The lady rang me about Beryl. Any reports were to be sent to the private address, not the office in town. I took the number straight down. You'd like a check with the telephone directory?"

Harries checked. I hadn't made a mistake.

"Right," Jewle said. "Get a picture of that number—" He broke off. "Get two pictures. One of the number and those immediately surrounding it: the other of the whole area of wall that's got numbers on it. If necessary we can blow them up later."

Harries left with his tail wagging.

"Fantastic!" Jewle said. "Just what we wanted. I only wish I'd had it half an hour ago."

It appeared he'd had a good conference up to a point. It couldn't be denied that some scheme or swindle had been worked and that Dorne had been killed in a quarrel over the proceeds, but that it might have been Lady Marport who'd paid out that money was something the Commander wasn't as yet prepared to believe. He thought any such implication, and, in fact, anything to do with her missing daughter, was a very long way from being proved. His final words had been something like this: "You establish the connection and then we'll decide about calling on Lady Marport. Until then, strictly nothing."

As Jewle said, most of that connection had now been established. Dorne had been in communication with the lady, and, unless he was interested in Home and Family, the telephone conversation could have been only about the missing daughter.

I asked him what he was going to do.

"See him again when the prints are ready. If that doesn't change his mind, I don't know what will."

"There may be some more for him," I said. "I'd meant to tell you as soon as I saw you this morning. All this excitement put it out of my mind."

If only in self-justification I told him what had made me wonder if Beryl by any chance had had a boy friend who might now know her whereabouts, and how I discovered there'd been one—David Prentiss.

"And he knew?"

"No," I said. "But two interesting pieces of information did emerge. The last time he met her was the Wednesday of Easter week, and the rendezvous was at two o'clock, at where do you think?"

He didn't even try to guess.

"Near the Silver Spoon! What's more, when she came out she was with Painter. She'd been having lunch with him."

He stared. "This is fantastic! Everything happening at once. Where do you think it gets us?"

"Not all that far. It definitely established a friendly connection between Beryl and Painter as long ago as last April. It isn't all that presumptuous to think he's known her whereabouts ever since she left home. And that the blackmail scheme we've only been guessing at is real hard fact."

"It's enough," he said. "Enough at least to interview the mother."

He glanced up at the clock. "Don't know about you but I'd like a cup of tea."

He rang through and in a couple of minutes in came a tray with the eternal British solace. He poured out a couple of cups.

"Let's go very slowly into the whole thing and then get it down on paper. You start with the missing daughter and we'll both go on from there."

We didn't even begin. There was a tap at the door. I often thought later it was rather like the knocking at the gate in *Macbeth*. A morning which we'd thought was over hadn't even begun.

A Sergeant McGill came in. I'd never met him but he was in Communications.

"Come in, sergeant," Jewle said. "What's bothering you?"

"This is, sir. It came by registered post this morning and we've been trying to track it down. Now we think it's yours." It was a small parcel, rather like a paper-backed book: in clean brown paper, neatly tied and sealing-waxed. The address, carefully printed, was this—

RE MISS M. WILSON

NEW SCOTLAND YARD

LONDON.

Jewle didn't turn a hair.

"It's mine all right. Wait a second and I'll give you a receipt." A minute later we were both looking down at that small parcel. It might have been a bomb.

"Right," he said. "Let's see what's in it."

He put on his gloves, found some scissors in a drawer and cut the string. With his thumbnail he carefully split the sealing-wax at the joint and turned the paper back.

What we now saw was a plain white envelope. Over it and tucked round the sides were two strips of cellophane.

"Good Lord!" I said. "It's what was underneath Dorne's desk. Whoever took it off tucked the cellophane round again."

"Better leave it for a minute," he said. "I'll try to get hold of Downing. We don't want to mess up any prints."

Luckily Downing was in. He came up in a couple of minutes. Jewle explained.

"We think there's something highly important in this envelope, so we'd like it printed. Pay special regard to three prints you already have—Molly Wilson's, Dorne's and the unknown woman whose prints were on Dorne's desk. You might also try the wrapping—just for luck."

He picked up the letter opener, discarded it and took out his pen-knife and felt the edge. With his gloved fingers he held the envelope down and carefully slit it open. He held it by a corner and shook, and with the knife he edged out what was in it—a collection of negatives. There were exactly a dozen.

"Right," he told Downing. "Make it a rush job and give me a ring when you've found something out."

We stood looking down at those negatives.

"Don't think prints'll matter," Jewle said, and picked one up.

He sat down and began manipulating the negative against the light. I don't know much about photography but I knew at least what he was doing. Get the light to fall in a certain way across a negative and it becomes positive, if only for a second or two while the light still holds a true angle.

"Good God!"

"What is it?"

"Unbelievable," he said. "Take a look for yourself and be prepared for a shock."

I began manipulating that negative till it was momentarily clear. One look and I dropped it.

"Horrible! Utterly horrible!"

"I know," he said. "It's not in your line. I spent a couple of years with the Vice Squad."

He thought for a moment, then picked up the receiver.

It was half an hour before the prints came up from the photographic lab, and they were brought up by an old friend of Jewle's—a Vice Squad inspector whose name was Horley. They were still damp and he laid them out on some blotting-paper on Jewle's desk.

One look was enough for me, but I could see they were a series. I don't regard myself as particularly moral or unaware of the dirtier facts of life, but even to think of those prints was a dirtying of one's own mind. I drew a bit back and started filling my pipe. The other two went on talking.

"What do you make of it?"

Horley took the glass.

"Looks like the corner of a *bidet*. It *is* a *bidet*."

"Then they're French. I doubt if you'd see a *bidet* here except in a brothel."

"Wait a minute," Horley said. "I've seen this set before."

The buzzer went. Jewle picked up the receiver. He listened for a minute and then hung up.

"Now where were we?"

"I was saying, I'm pretty sure we have some of these. The last lot we had was after a raid at Limehouse. It might pay to make sure."

He went out. Jewle picked up the glass and bent down. He gave a curious sort of grunt and shifted position. He looked again.

"Have a peep," he told me. "I don't think you're going to like it, but take a look."

I looked. A naked man and a naked woman on a bed. The man was backwards but the woman was full-faced. I hadn't a moment's doubt about who she was.

"I don't believe it! She just couldn't."

"I told you you wouldn't like it. Still, there it is."

"But it runs counter to everything I've ever heard about her. It's sheer filth. Utterly degrading."

"Take a look at some of the others. They're worse still. By the way, that was Downing ringing. He's established two sets of prints: Dorne's and the unknown woman's. The woman was the one who sent the package."

"Then she couldn't have been Beryl Marport."

"Don't know," he said. "In spite of the fact that it was her, she might have had some special reason. She may even have wanted us to know."

He frowned. "In any case, I don't like it. If she was used to take these photographs, I'm wondering if she was even allowed to live."

"No," I said. "No. They couldn't have done that!"

"Dorne was killed? You might have been killed? What's one killing more or less?"

Horley came back. He was looking pretty pleased with himself.

"I was right," he said. "They're one of the best-known series: docketed as Marseilles 3. They've been on the market about three years. Let me have a look at the woman again." He had a good look and he wasn't so happy.

"Well, I'm damned! You have a look."

Jewle looked.

"By God, you're right! The same man and everything but not the same woman!"

He handed me the glass. Now I knew more or less what to expect, I wasn't so squeamish. They were right. In those two sets of prints everything was identical—the bed, the side of a *bidet*, a glimpse of a brass rod and a rail, the man and the position of the bodies. The only thing different was the head of the woman. In the French set she wasn't even remotely like Beryl Marport.

"Just a clever bit of faking," Horley said.

I asked him how he'd have done it himself.

"I couldn't," he said. "It was an expert job. First of all someone studied very carefully the exact position of—let's call her Marianne—of Marianne's head. Then the other woman was photographed in just the right attitudes—just the head—and the substitution made. Negatives were made and touched up and tested, and even made again and again till the substitution couldn't be detected, and Bob was your uncle."

A word or two more and he left.

"Marler!" Jewle said before the door had hardly closed. "He was the expert. Painter got Beryl to sit for him on some pretext or other, then Dorne was brought in and he operated the blackmail scheme."

"And Beryl wouldn't know."

"I very much doubt it. I think you were right. I think it'd have taken a much thicker skin than hers to have knowingly got involved in that sort of thing."

He waved a contemptuous hand at the prints.

"No wonder the mother paid up," I said. "At meetings she used occasionally to refer to her daughter, probably as a kind of shining example."

Jewle didn't seem to be listening.

"That's it," he said. "It pieces everything together."

"What does?"

"What Dorne was up to. His own little private scheme. Don't you see? He managed to get hold of the negatives and taped them under his desk for security. Later he was going to get in touch with Lady Marport again. 'Sorry, but what you bought was only the set of prints. Now you have to buy the negatives and make sure there aren't any more.'"

"And that was why he was killed?"

"One of the reasons. We've got to take the blackmail money into account too. That three thousand we recovered couldn't have been his legitimate share or he wouldn't have had to park it at Charing Cross."

"And the unknown woman who collected the envelope of negatives from Dorne's office and then sent them here. What about her? Whoever she was she knew Molly Wilson or she wouldn't have used her name on the address."

"I know," he said. "But there's more to it than that. Why mention Molly at all? She's most unlikely to have had anything to do with that blackmail business. I can't see her doing any more than keeping that left-luggage receipt for Dorne."

"But would Painter or whoever it was have beaten her up for that? Wouldn't the missing negatives have been more important? Perhaps they weren't Dorne's private scheme. They might have been a follow-up by all the gang."

Jewle threw in his hand. "Let's leave it. We might go on arguing all day. We're too close to everything. Better sleep on it and see how it looks tomorrow. I'll stand you a lunch."

We didn't go to the Silver Spoon. I guessed he wasn't in the mood for running across Painter. We went to that little place in Westminster instead.

We'd been late at lunch and it was well after two when we got back. There was a message for Jewle from somewhere up top and I left too. It had been a through-other kind of day as they say up North: almost all of it good. Something like Christmas.

I said I left. That wasn't quite true. Just outside the door I almost collided with Downing who was bringing Jewle pictures of the prints on that morning's package. I went back inside with him and recognised a chance of getting something for nothing—a kind of free advanced course on prints. Luckily for me he wasn't in any hurry.

Length and width, plus long experience, made him sure the prints were a woman's. Then he began pointing out ridge characteristics, with variations of ending and forking, and the short, independent ridges or islands. Since the characteristics were not confined to any particular area, even a fragment might be sufficient to establish identity. He himself didn't need to pattern a whole print:

there'd be sufficient permutations of characteristics in any reasonably sized area.

Most of those technicalities I'd learned from the text-books. What I'd never had was so practical a demonstration: in fact, by the time it was over I'd have been prepared to bet I could have spotted those prints among a score of others in almost the wink of an eye.

I spent the rest of the afternoon at the agency, trying to get back into touch with things. When I got home that early evening there was almost an hour to go to the meal. I wasn't sorry. I wanted to test my newly acquired skills.

I didn't need any apparatus: just those two prints I'd taken from the letter Beryl had written to her mother; a ruler and a sharply pointed pencil. What Downing had done was to draw a thin line from a characteristic to outside the print and give it the corresponding letter and continue till he had enough either to characterise or verify the actual print.

I'd drawn and lettered a couple of ridge characteristics when all at once I had something like a cold sweat. I put the glass on that print, searched it and then I was blinking away as if I'd just woken from a nap.

I looked at my watch. Downing would be long since gone, so I wrote a quick explanatory note, put it and the prints into an envelope and addressed it. I told Bernice I might be a minute or two late, hustled on my overcoat and nipped down the stairs. At Leicester Square I took a ticket for Westminster and walked from there to the Yard. I came back the same way and was home just before seven.

It was to be a queer sort of evening. The programme I should have been watching on television ought to have been fascinating, but I couldn't concentrate. In one way it turned out to be all for the best. That may sound enigmatical but you'll have to wait for the explanation.

Bernice was saying she hadn't enjoyed a programme so much for a long time. I hypocritically agreed.

"But I do think," she said, "that they shouldn't have had Brenda Holt so heavily made up. She can make a play just by being in it."

"But she was supposed to be an old woman."

"Of course," she said. "But it ruined all the facial gestures. She can say more with her face than most actresses can with their lines."

Mercifully or unmercifully the telephone went. Jewle was ringing me to say the Wimbledon visit had been definitely fixed for Wednesday morning at nine-thirty. It had been accepted that I ought to be there and so, if I didn't hear anything to the contrary, he'd pick me up at eight-thirty.

And so virtually ended an eventful day. I'd hoped to get quickly to sleep: as it was it must have been well over an hour before I managed to drop off. The questions were there and I just had to find answers.

Why in heaven's name had it been Beryl Marport who had taken that envelope from Dorne's office and then sent it to the Yard with the knowledge that it concerned Molly Wilson? Had she known the real contents of that envelope? Had she been a party to the blackmail? Where was she? Was she Painter's mistress and stashed away in some apartment?

There were even more questions. I guess that at last it was sheer mental exhaustion that left nothing but sleep.

CHAPTER 14
GREAT MORNING

I'D EXPECTED Downing or Jewle to ring me. It was about ten o'clock when Jewle did ring me at the agency. He said Downing had just shown him my letter and the Beryl Marport prints.

"I just can't believe it," he said. "I'd begun to think the damn woman never existed. You any ideas yourself?"

In view of that overnight sleepless hour and the fact that my subconscious had gone on strike, that was definitely ironic.

"Well, no point in trying to argue it out," he said. "Let me know if you *do* get any ideas. In any case I'll be seeing you in the morning at half-past eight."

The trouble was that I had plenty of ideas. Individually they might make sense: put two or three together and they made sheer nonsense, so what I tried to do that day was to keep the whole thing from my mind. I must have partially succeeded: at least I wasn't too long in getting to sleep.

Jewle had allowed a full hour because of morning traffic, and we needed most of it. We hung around for only ten minutes before pushing the bell. It was my old friend May Forster, the housekeeper, who admitted us. A few seconds and we were entering the lounge.

I'd expected to see a change in Dora Marport but there was nothing I could discern. She was just her old assured and imperious self. There was a kind of condescending dignity in the way she held out a hand to Jewle. I was slightly in the background and she'd blinked just a bit at the first sight of me, but I didn't get a handshake.

"Nice to see you again, Mr. Travers. What this is about, Superintendent, I can't imagine, unless you have some news about my daughter. But please sit down."

We got settled. Jewle went straight into the attack. He took something from his brief-case and passed it across the desk.

"Lady Marport, have you ever seen this man?"

There was something slightly supercilious in the way she looked at it.

"Never," she said. "I never saw him in my life. Who is he?"

"But surely you read the newspapers? There was a photograph of him there."

"I'm afraid I get little time. My secretary goes through them for me. She's been with me a very long time and knows what might interest me."

"Then let me tell you something about him," Jewle said. "He was fished out of the Thames with a knife wound in his back. In his possession was quite a large sum of money: the proceeds of a blackmail scheme he and two others had just brought off. His name was Leonard Dorne."

"Indeed? But why should any of this concern me? I've never even heard the wretched man's name."

"I believe you. Names are just names. But this. Don't be shocked when you look at it, but have you seen anything like it before? Have a close look at the woman, Lady Marport. She's your own daughter."

He gave her the print. A look and she dropped it. She flushed angrily.

"This is disgraceful! I shall inform your superiors. I've never been so shamed in all my life."

"You do that, Lady Marport," Jewle said. "They expect you to. If you wish to get me into any trouble, tell them I *didn't* show you that photograph, because it was on their express orders that I did."

"I don't believe it. I *can't* believe it."

"Then ring," Jewle said. "I'll give you the special number." She sat tight-lipped.

"Very well, Why *did* you show me this—this thing?"

Jewle's smile was conciliatory. "Because we have your interests at heart. We don't want any notoriety."

"Notoriety?" The sideways look was one of amazement. "I don't understand."

"Right," Jewle said. "Am I to take it you decline absolutely to co-operate?"

Her hands lifted and fell. "Co-operate in what? So far all you've done is mention a man I've never even heard of and show me—well, this disgusting thing."

"You've seen such things before. You've been campaigning against pornography for years. You must have seen them."

He got to his feet and turned to me. "We'll see the bank manager about the used five-pound notes, then go on to Fleet Street."

"Wait a moment," she said. "What five-pound notes?"

Jewle sat down again. "I've no time to waste, Lady Marport. I present you with two alternatives. You co-operate fully with us or tomorrow morning the whole story will be in the press: how you submitted to blackmail and why." He reached across for the print. "You won't need this. It'll be in the papers too." He got to his feet. "Co-operate with us and the whole thing will be kept confidential. I give you my solemn word on that. So will

Mr. Travers. But no shilly-shallying. You won't be able to bring us back. Once we leave this room we go straight to Fleet Street."

He got up again. I followed suit. He waited for maybe half a minute.

"Please don't trouble to ring," he said quietly. "We'll let ourselves out."

He moved towards the door and then it suddenly happened. I'd never have believed it possible. It was so utterly out of character and yet there she was: head on arms and sobbing her heart out. Jewle looked at me and nodded towards the door.

I rapped on the side door in the entrance hall. May Forster looked out, face wrinkling in a smile.

"Ah, you're going, sir?"

I told her it was Lady Marport. She'd had an upset. Maybe she ought to rest for a bit. Till she recovered we'd just wait.

May had literally led her out. Later she'd brought us coffee. It wasn't anything serious, she said. Her ladyship had had some sort of upset. She'd stirred the fire to a cheerful blaze and left.

Another quarter of an hour and her ladyship appeared. What followed was about as awkward—if you know what I mean—as anything I'd known in my life. But we got the story.

She's been rung at Croft House by a man who said he had some information which would interest her. He was a private detective who'd been working on a case and had learned in the course of it that a couple of men had got into touch with her daughter and were going in some way to compromise her. He said his name was Johnson. If he heard more he'd ring her again. Meanwhile, he'd go on making enquiries.

He'd given her little chance to talk. The following evening he'd rung again. He said the two blackmailers were prepared, since he now knew all about it, to let him act as go-between. What they had were some compromising pictures of her daughter and he'd managed to get hold of one and would put it in the post at once. Meanwhile, it would be very dangerous either to go to the police or anyone else. The only way to handle things was the way he was handling them himself.

Then he'd rung off. The print duly arrived the next morning. The climax came when he rang the same evening. Unless Lady Marport was prepared to pay the sum of five thousand pounds, preferably in used five-pound notes, copies of similar prints would be posted to every member of Home and Family. Also she was going to be watched in case she went to the police. Those were the best terms he'd been able to get.

She was given three days to have the money ready. On the evening of the third day—the Saturday—she was to have the money in a parcel and go to the gate at six-thirty. There a man would meet her, hand over the prints and take the money. Which was exactly what happened. It was practically dark by the gate and she hadn't seen much of the man. All she'd known was that he was quite tall.

Jewle thanked her. No upbraidings about not having gone to the police. No reprimands or recriminations— just thanks.

"This is the last you'll hear about it," he said. "Nothing will ever be made public. We've already recovered three thousand pounds and that will be returned to you confidentially, as will anything else. Forget all about it, Lady Marport; leave everything to us. We think we know who the men are but we shan't even require you as a witness."

She called to me as I was nearing the door. "Mr. Travers, I'm ashamed to say this, but what about my daughter? Will you now go on trying to find her?"

"Of course," I said. "She may be found very soon. But believe what we told you. She was absolutely unaware of all this."

We sat for a moment or two before Jewle moved the car off.

"You got the full implications?" he said. "Dorne collected the money that Saturday night and he later turned up at Painter's place in time to em-cee that pop affair. But when he turned up at the rendezvous later on, he had only two thousand pounds. The balance was at Charing Cross. What the excuse was we shan't know till someone tells us."

I said it must have been some sort of double crossing, which was why he was killed. And that same night. Or the very early hours of the following morning.

"We'll soon know," he told me confidently. "Marler's the weak link. He's the one who'll talk. But not yet."

He moved the car on. He'd asked if I wanted to be set down at the agency. I said it was ridiculous to take me on through the city traffic. From Wimbledon Station I could be there in a quarter the time.

So he pulled in. As I was about to get out he had a last word.

"I'm not supposed to tell you this, but what may be some important developments are booked for tonight.

Don't ask me any questions. If things turn out as hoped, in the morning I'll give you a ring."

It was about half-past nine the next morning when he rang me. He said nothing about those mysterious developments: merely asked if I could get along to the Yard. I said I'd be there as soon as I could make it.

The weather hadn't changed so much as worsened. A sleety rain was lashing the windows of Jewle's room, the room itself felt on the chilly side but Jewle himself was looking as if the voice of the turtle was heard in the land.

"I seem to've got you here a bit early," he said. "Make yourself comfortable. At any moment now we ought to have some news."

"About those developments you mentioned?"

"Oh, that," he said. "That was just the beginning. It wasn't my job at all, though I did make one suggestion."

The smile had a touch of the self-congratulatory.

"Let me ask you a question. Molly Wilson wasn't in the coffee bar on Wednesday and Saturday nights. Painter was. Why?"

"Simply because there was always the possibility of something getting out of hand on the dance floor. The bad apples in the barrel, so to speak, and Dorne was a better man for handling things than Painter."

There was another smile. "You really believe that? Which one would you back if it came to a fight?"

"You're right," I said. "You tell me. Why *did* Painter take over the counter on Wednesday and Saturday nights?"

"Because it's only over the counter that you sell things. See the point?"

"I don't think you could say I was right," he went on. "I just saw Painter from a different angle. Now I'll tell you exactly what happened last night. It wasn't my pigeon: I was there because I was an interested party. To get to the point, there was a full-scale raid on Painter's place last night with a warrant under the Dangerous Drugs Act. The whole place was sealed off in a few seconds. Selected teenagers were searched and eleven have already appeared in court. Six admitted possession and were fined: the other five were accused and remanded. Painter himself was pulled in and bail's being opposed. That was the plum I wanted out of the pie: just to get him on a holding charge while we take another look or two around."

I must have chuckled. "Wonderful! Couldn't be better. And it was that Pop Night business that gave you the idea?"

"Only to mention it to those concerned. There was also the matter of Painter and his money. Peddling is a mighty profitable business, especially if you get the goods free. He'd start in a small way and make plumb sure. News would gradually get around and he'd get to know his regulars, but it always had to be something he handled himself."

There was a tap at the door. Harries was showing someone in: someone whom I vaguely recognised.

"You know Mr. Bland?" Jewle said.

"Of course!" I held out my hand. "Last October. That robbery with violence at that place of yours at Stepney."

"Sit down," Jewle said. "Make yourself at home. A cigarette?"

He had one himself. I got my pipe going.

"Now tell us the worst," Jewle said.

Bland smiled. "The best, you mean. I've positively identified the goods as coming from us: the heroin pills particularly."

"That's fine," Jewle said. "Now I can tell you something: where exactly all the stuff was found. Travers, you remember that handsome desk in Painter's office? It looked to me as if it had been especially made. And so it had. Three of the large drawers didn't go all the way back. We found the stuff in the spaces: secret drawers, if you like."

Bland said he'd check with the amount stolen. If he was asked to give a rough idea he'd say about half had been recovered. He'd get busy with it at once.

"Wait a minute," Jewle said. "There's something else."

He smiled. "You people must have thought us fools at the time, so you ought to know what else we found. We suggested, you remember, that the likeliest way of entry was by posing as police officers. Well, in one of the compartments of that desk we found the uniform of a police inspector: all nicely rolled up and ready if wanted."

I wasn't so dumb as not to see the implications. As soon as Bland left I put the question to Jewle.

"Painter and Dorne did that robbery?"

"Almost certainly."

"So you needn't worry so much about the murder of Dorne. Since you've proof of the robbery, then either Dorne or Painter must have killed the night watchman."

"That's more or less right," he said. "At any rate, we've got more than enough to hold Painter till we're absolutely ready. But about the murder of Dorne. There're a couple of other things. Dorne wasn't dangerous only because he was demanding a bigger share of that five thousand pounds and was under suspicion of having taken those negatives: he was also dangerous in two other ways to Painter, that is. He knew about the drug traffic and probably took his regular cut. He also knew that it was Painter who coshed the nightwatchman. Slipping a knife into him solved a lot of problems."

"True enough," I said. "And what now?"

He was grinning as he got to his feet.

"We'll have a little chat with friend Marler. Just enough to scare him. Might have to pull him in for questioning. It'll all depend."

Harries and I sat at the back. Jewle drove. It was about half-past eleven when we drew up near Marler's place. Harries stayed: Jewle and I walked in. Once more we found Marler in his office. He was wary but less so, perhaps, than before.

"Just passing," Jewle said, and helped himself to a chair. "Wondered if you'd heard the bad news."

Marler stared. There was something chameleon-like about that beard of his. Now it was giving a touch of the pathetic.

"Your brother. You haven't heard?"

"No," he said, and I believed him. "What bad news?"

"He's been peddling drugs."

"Peddling drugs?" He shook his head. "I can't believe it. Why would he want to do that?"

"The same reason why you're in here this morning," Jewle said amiably. "To make money. At any rate he was caught in the act. By now he'll have been remanded without bail. He may get off with two years. I doubt it though. Besides, there's that other charge."

He waited for the questioning look.

"That's right. The murder of Dorne. Didn't I ask you about that before?"

"I told you and this gentleman here I knew nothing about it."

"So you did. Must have slipped my mind. By the way, what was your reaction when Dorne demanded more than half of that five thousand?"

It hit him clean in the wind. Even if it hadn't you can always tell. If you're the watcher, that is. An over-dose of insouciance, perhaps, or too much indignation. All Marler managed to ask was what five thousand.

"Probably something else they didn't tell you about," Jewle said. "Which reminds me."

He looked at me. "We forgot to offer Mr. Marler our congratulations."

"It's not too late," I said.

"You're right. One of the neatest photographic jobs I ever saw."

Marler took the print. A second or two and he was as good as thrusting it back into Jewle's hand.

"No, Superintendent. I'd never get mixed up with that sort of thing. I keep my business strictly clean. I'm a married man with a couple of children."

It was so irrelevant I almost laughed.

Jewle kept a straight face. "I'd forgotten that."

He put the print carefully back in his wallet.

"Just twelve little prints," he said. "Five thousand pounds. And the lady didn't turn a hair at over four hundred a print. You know something, Mr. Marler? I'm beginning to think I'm in the wrong business."

Marler didn't know whether or not to smile.

"Twelve prints," Jewle went on. "You can buy them in sets for as little as ten bob, if you're that-way minded. Which reminds me again. Did you know, Mr. Marler, that Dorne did have the negatives? No wonder your brother couldn't find them. They were in an envelope taped under his desk."

It may seem obvious or even crude to you, but I was watching Marler's face. Jewle was leading him round in circles. Disjointed circles. Marler didn't know what was coming next.

"Must have scared you stiff. Your own brother and Dorne. And having to get rid of the body. What should have been a nice, friendly meeting ending like that. I can imagine the shock."

Marler's hands were quivering. "Superintendent, please! I don't know what you're talking about. I told you so before. You just said you believed me. This gentleman heard you."

"That's right," I said. "But Mr. Marler surely wouldn't mind telling us where he was that particular night?"

"I was at home. Ask my wife, Superintendent. She can prove it. I always am on a Saturday night."

Jewle relaxed. He even smiled. "Now that's very interesting. How did you know it took place on a Saturday night? How will your wife know which Saturday night? I think you'd better come along with us and help us with the enquiries."

He almost cringed.

"But I can't," he said. "What about my business? I've got a client at two o'clock."

"Tell your secretary on the way out," Jewle said.

A couple of minutes and we were walking towards the car. Jewle suddenly stopped.

"We should have told that secretary of yours that you might be away quite a time. Might be even two or three days."

Marler's face had a sudden look of fright. "But my wife? I've got to get in touch with my wife." He drew himself up. "You can't do this to me, Superintendent."

"We'll get into touch with your wife," Jewle said quietly. "Might be only two hours. Might be two weeks. Depends on whether or not you're prepared to talk."

He moved Marler on. I opened the rear door and Marler joined Harries. I took the front seat and Jewle started to back the car. At the Yard he and Harries took Marler in. I was asked to stay put. It was only a minute or two before Jewle was back.

"What now?" I said.

"Well, in view of developments, I thought of trying another talk with Molly Wilson. You like to come along or shall I have a car take you somewhere?"

I said I'd go along.

This time I stayed in the car. Jewle said he had just two questions to ask and, Lambert permitting, everything could be over in five minutes.

The rain was coming down but the heater had been on and it was snug in that car. Jewle was away much longer than his five minutes. Maybe he'd had trouble from Lambert. Not that I minded. It had been a good morning and my pipe was going well.

When he did come back he wasn't looking too pleased.

"I saw her easily enough," he said, "but she isn't ready to talk—not yet. When I told her about Painter I said to myself, 'This is it,' but it wasn't." He shook his head. "That woman's got too many problems. Can't put my finger on anything unless she's still shielding somebody. Who the devil it could be I can't think."

"Wait a minute," I said. "She might have known about those negatives and sent Beryl for them. Just an idea."

"Molly Wilson knew Beryl Marport!" He snorted. "They weren't in the same class. If she knew anything about her it could only have been through Painter, and you think Painter would have told her? Far as he was concerned, she was just a waitress."

"A waitress who was friendly with Dorne."

"Even Dorne wouldn't have known," he said. "I'll bet you anything you like that Dorne didn't come into that scheme till the very last moment: in fact when the pictures were absolutely ready. His job was to use them. He'd have no idea who the girl in the pictures was.

"And another thing," he went on. "Dorne may have been living with Wilson but do you think he'd have told her the kind of crook he was? She's a good, honest, straight-forward sort of woman. Enjoyed a bit of fun with Dorne but nothing else. Do you know something else I think? If she'd had even an idea Dorne was a crook she'd have turned him out."

I said he was probably right. Just as his hand went down to the foot-brake I said something else.

"Remember I promised Lady Marport to do something about Beryl again. Looks as if you won't be wanting me much more so that's what I have to start concentrating on. I take it you'll lend a hand if you can?"

He said he certainly would. Whatever cropped up he'd immediately pass on. In any case, as he said, I now knew a lot more. Taking those negatives and sending them to the Yard, for instance. Also Marler, the weak link, might soon talk. He'd seen a lot of Beryl when he'd been taking those head and neck photographs.

He moved the car on. I sat thinking about Beryl Marport: trying to go back to the beginning and working things out from there. And then something like a miracle happened. We'd gone back by way of Tottenham Court Road, and, towards the far end we were held up in a jam. It was as I was looking about me that I saw a name on a shop front.

"Mind if I get out here?" I suddenly said. "I've just remembered. Some shopping I had to do. I'll walk to the flat."

CHAPTER 15
THE WANDERER

PERMIT me a digression. You may be wondering why I made that hasty exit from Jewle's car, so I'll tell you in my own roundabout way.

You probably think the profession of private investigator is an easy enough one to follow. You may go further and think that with an office, the necessary reference books and advertisements in suitable papers you could do pretty well at the job yourself. Also disguises would be fun and trailing an adventure. Maybe you'd be right.

Or you might think *profession* the wrong word. A private detective—even an expert like Hallows—isn't the result of schooling, as is a doctor or lawyer. He picks up his trade as he goes along in what's known as the school of experience. If so, and he's been born with a certain flair, he's learned quite a lot by the way: when to talk and when not: when to lie, to threaten, to cajole and when not. He has to interpret a gesture or look and discern in the haystack of words the needle of truth. Or it may be the other way round. He has to learn a score of other things and he's always learning.

His greatest asset is a first-class memory. There are two kinds: what I might call the factual and obvious, like the whereabouts of a place, the name of a person or the essential facts of a conversation. The other comes from long experience, or you may have been so lucky as to have been born with it. It consists of storing in some mental reservoir things heard and seen and to be able to draw on them—like turning on a tap—at the necessary moment.

The sight of Elwood's shop was such a moment: what I might call the moment of impetus. You remember Elwood? The man with whom I spent an hour in the coffee bar the night I was coshed? He was the reason and, as soon as Jewle's car had moved on, I walked into the shop.

He spotted me at once and waved away the assistant who'd approached me. I asked after Nora, his young daughter. She was in bed with a cold. I was glad in a way. It meant she had missed the previous Pop Night. Elwood himself knew nothing about the raid or he'd have mentioned it.

Bernice had been telling me for some time that I was running short of socks, so I bought half-a-dozen pairs and a couple of Ascot ties. While he was making up the package he asked if I'd recently been to the coffee bar. It gave me the opening. I said there'd been something I'd been meaning to ask him for quite a time. Did he remember my showing him and Nora a photograph of my niece? The one who occasionally turned up at Pop Nights? And how both of them had hesitated for a moment when they'd looked at the photograph?

He remembered, so I asked him why. He didn't hesitate for a moment about his answer.

I walked a few yards back and had a very scratch meal at a milk bar. It was half-past one when I came out and I went straight to Tempest Street. I wasn't altogether surprised when I found the coffee bar closed.

I walked round to the main entrance in Sandown Street and the doors were closed too. I pushed the bell and waited. I pushed it again and heard a faint sound. A moment and the door opened. Tessa Brooks was looking as if she couldn't care less.

"It's you," she said. "Sorry, but we're closed."

"I know," I said. "I've heard about it. It's rough on you people."

She beckoned me in and closed the door behind me.

"Mr. Painter: what's going to happen to him? You ought to know."

"A year or two in jail," I said. "If I were you I'd start looking for a new job. What're you doing here now?"

"Someone had to answer telephone calls. You're not kidding me about him going to jail?"

"Read the evening paper," I told her. "It shouldn't worry you. With your looks and ability you could get another job in no time. What I came for was to see Susan Farley. She isn't here?"

"Nobody's here but me."

"You could let me have her address?"

She hesitated. She shrugged her shoulders.

"Wait here a minute."

I waited three minutes. She gave me a sheet of paper on which was the address.

"What do you want her address for? Was she mixed up in this?"

I raised a secretive hand. "Just between ourselves that's what I want to find out."

A sort of nod for silence and I slipped back out. As soon as I'd turned the corner I looked at the address.

Miss S. Farley,
     23 Mayes Court,
          Holloway.

I walked back to Tottenham Court Road Station. I left the train at Holloway Road and started making enquiries. It was a postman who finally put me on the right track. Five minutes and I was taking a look at an apartment block. Demolition work was going on just up the road, and it looked as if Mayes Court too was over-ripe for development. It had that kind of look. Pre-Edwardian is practically a millennium back.

Everything was neat and tidy inside. At the desk a rather plump young woman was knitting and reading and the needles stopped clicking only when she turned a page. That's no great feat. Bernice can read, knit and watch television.

I smiled down at her. "Number twenty-three?"

She smiled back. "Second floor. The lift's on the right."

It was a self-service lift. The carpeting along the passage was well-worn. Pop music, muted by a closed door, was coming from Number 19. Number 23 was just by it, on my left and I could still hear music. It was Bach, but I couldn't just place it.

Maybe a Brandenburg Concerto. I could never remember the numbers.

I rang. The music suddenly stopped. A moment and the door was open. There was a quick look of recognition. She was fairly far back from the door so I didn't ask for permission. I stepped just inside.

"Sorry to disturb you like this but I've been looking for you for a very long time."

She frowned. "Your name's Blake. I saw you at Mr. Marler's place."

"You did," I said. "Then you were Susan Farley. Now you're Beryl Marport."

She stared. She must have seen the faint smile because she suddenly smiled too. Then she laughed.

"You'd better come in. Nothing of that matters now. Everything's gone haywire, or didn't you know?"

She was wearing a brown pullover and dark yellow slacks that accentuated the slimness of the legs. There was something graceful in the way she closed the door and followed me into the room. That photograph had almost slandered her. I'd rarely seen a face more attractive.

"My name's actually Travers," I said. "I'm a private enquiry agent, working for your mother."

She looked surprised. "I don't want to be rude, but you don't look like one."

"I know," I said. "Between ourselves, that's why I took so long finding you."

"Well, sit down," she said, "And do take off that coat."

I sat on the settee. Heating made the room quite warm and a gas-fire was burning in the recess where there had once been a grate. To my left was a radiogram and by it a huge stack of records. In the other corner was a television set. The furnishings looked somewhat worn but the room itself was snug enough and well-lighted.

She had taken a chair. The quizzical look was still there.

"Tell me about it," she said. "How did you find me?"

"It's a long story. The red hair didn't help. I'd never seen you and I'd only the usual black-and-white photograph to go on. Then that morning in Marler's office you'd deliberately left a lot of make-up on and it aged you. The slight Cockney accent fooled me too. On the whole I'd say you put up an uncommonly good show."

She laughed. "Yes, but how *did* you find me?"

"It's still a long story. I didn't know till late this morning and then I remembered a whole lot of things. One was a talk I had with David Prentiss—"

"David! You saw David!"

"On a Sunday morning at Little Warfield. His people were at church and he was cleaning his car. He told me about those winter term dances you used to have at St. Winifred's. Practically old-time dances. Since you appeared to have been good at most things, I should have guessed you were good at them."

"I was," she said. "But David. How was he?"

"In great shape. He's a nice boy, Beryl. You ought to marry him."

She smiled. "Maybe I will. But do go on. What else did you find out?"

"The final thing was this morning. I was in your coffee bar one evening and got talking to a former old-time client. It was a Pop Night and he was chaperoning his young daughter, so I showed them the photograph and said it was my niece. They both hesitated a bit before they said they'd never seen you. This morning I ran across the man again and I asked why the hesitation. He said there'd been quite a resemblance to Susan Farley who took the old-time dancing class. So I went to the academy just now and managed to get her address."

She nodded approvingly. "All the same, that was very clever of you. I'm sorry I said you didn't look like a detective."

"It's still true," I said, and gave a look round. "This apartment must be costing you quite a lot?"

"The top apartments come cheaper. This one is about five hundred."

I stared. "How do you manage? You couldn't have had much more than a hundred when you left home."

"Oh, but I've been doing quite well. Painter didn't pay all that much but there was also modelling fairly often for Marler. Also I share the apartment with another girl. She works in a bank. An awfully nice girl. We get along fine."

I had to laugh and she asked me why. I said it reminded me of the story of the man who'd retired from some small business or other and someone asked him how he'd managed it. He said he'd made a bit here and a bit there, and the questioner said that didn't account for it. 'Oh' said the man. 'I forgot to tell you an aunt died and left me twenty thousand pounds.'

She laughed. There was a lot of April about her, and it went.

"Let me get you some tea. I know it's early but I feel like some myself."

I said that'd be fine and she jumped up at once. I sat on, thinking things over, but mostly I thought about her. Everything about her had character: her movements, the way she spoke, even the self-composure.

She brought in a tray. I placed a small table for her.

"Afraid there's only biscuits," she said. "We both of us have tea out."

"Cosy here," I said as I sipped my tea. "Which reminds me. Isn't it time you did some talking. How did you happen to meet Painter, for instance?"

"It was Ellen Moore," she said. "She and I were rather friendly at school, and when an American uncle of hers was over here and asked her to lunch in town, she wanted me to go with her. It was at a place called the Silver Spoon and we had a sherry at the bar before lunch, and Painter was there. He and the uncle got talking. You know how impulsive and generous Americans are. At any rate, Painter was asked to join us. That's when I heard all about the academy he was running. That's how it all started. I'd already begun to think of leaving mother so I called on him. What happened was that during the rest of that holiday I took a refresher course and he was really awfully pleased with me. He said if there was an opening he'd be glad to employ me. I saw him again at half-term and he thought there'd be a vacancy early in September. He also put me in touch with Marler."

"And as soon as you left home you began working?"

"Well, I had to find this place. And buy some suitable clothes and have my hair dyed. Painter liked it that way. Just as he thought it a good thing to change my name."

"And you'd previously told him all about yourself?"

She laughed. "But of course! He was a snob. And it helped me get the job."

"Strikes me as a very convenient opening," I said. "No strings attached?"

She flushed slightly. "At first, yes. He even suggested getting a nicer apartment for me. I was pretty sure he was going to sack me after I told him I just wasn't that kind, but he didn't. I oughtn't to say so but I was really quite good. And he was paying me less than the girl whose place I took."

She hesitated. She smiled. "Also he happened to engage a new receptionist. Everyone knew they got along fine."

"That'd be Tessa Brooks?"

She smiled again, claws showing. "She was a horrible creature, really. The only one there I really disliked."

"But you were happy there?"

"Of course! I couldn't have had anything nicer, even right in town. And everyone was friendly." She frowned. "Painter was a bit of a blight and I wasn't so keen on modelling for Marler, but otherwise it was simply perfect."

"What was Molly Wilson like?"

"Oh, I liked her enormously. She was so natural. Everyone was shocked when they knew the awful thing that had happened to her."

I didn't tell her I was the one who gave her the news over the telephone.

"And Leonard Dorne," I said. "The man who was murdered. Did you know him?"

"Only very slightly. Everyone knew, of course, that he and Molly had—well, an arrangement."

I set down the cup. Tea, I said, had been just what I'd wanted.

"Now I've got to talk to you seriously," I said. "About Molly Wilson and Dorne and yourself. I had your finger-prints. I took them from the last letter you wrote to your mother. The same prints were on Dorne's desk. And on a package that had been cellophaned under it and later sent to Scotland Yard. Hadn't you better tell me about it?"

For a moment she was very still. "I'm in trouble with the police?"

"No," I said. "This is between you and me. Just tell me about it."

It was what I should have guessed. On the Saturday evening Molly had actually come to see her. She was worried about Dorne.

"It was hard to get anything out of her. I thought she was hiding something. Not telling me the truth. Then she told me about the package and would I fetch it and keep it till she asked for it. She gave me the key and on the Sunday morning I just let myself in and took it. Then when I heard what had happened to her, I thought I'd better send it to the police."

I opened up a bit more. "This is also strictly between our two selves, but Dorne was a bad egg. He was black-mailing someone and on the Saturday evening he was collecting the money. But he didn't know or couldn't be absolutely certain that the person hadn't informed the police, so what he said to Molly was something like this. 'If I'm not back at a certain time, you take this key and collect a certain package.' Molly was scared to go herself so she came to you."

It wasn't the whole truth. I wasn't dead sure of the truth myself, but it was near enough.

"Painter was a bad egg, too," I said. "A drug pedlar. You heard about the raid last night?"

"Yes," she said. "Everything was shut up this morning when I arrived, so I rang up one of the girls and she told me."

"And now Othello's occupation's gone."

"I'm not worrying," she said. "Not yet. I'm pretty sure I could get another job. I've made quite a lot of friends."

"And what's your ultimate ambition? Other than getting married?"

She laughed. "I'd like to have my own place. Small but select, if you know what I mean. It might be in one of the nicer suburbs."

"And nothing else first? Like going back home?"

"No!" She almost snapped the word. "Not yet. I can't go back to that sort of thing. You must have formed your own idea of what it was like." She shook her head again. "Some time, perhaps. I don't know."

"You're right," I said. "You're entitled to your own life. The last few weeks have proved it. So let me talk to you like a father. Heaven knows I'm old enough."

She actually smiled.

"You're also part of your mother's life. I saw her very recently and she's changed quite a lot. I'm not just saying that. I'm sure you'd find everything different. I don't ask you to go back to Croft House and do whatever she wants for you. What I ask you to do is get in real touch with her. See her and put your case. I think you'll be astonished at the way she'll take it. If you aren't too proud, or merely obstinate, she might finance that new place you've been thinking about. Until you get your own money."

She listened quietly, knees drawn up on the chair and arms round them.

"I don't know. The way you put it—Well, maybe I will. But you won't say anything to her? Tell her where I am?"

"Not a word. Everything has to be up to you."

I got to my feet and said I'd really have to be going. She insisted on holding the overcoat for me.

"It's been nice," she said. "I ought to thank you but I don't know how."

Then as I turned, her hands were suddenly on my shoulders. She tip-toed up and just managed to kiss my cheek. I had to laugh.

"All debts paid," I told her. "One of these days I might drop in again."

On the top of a slow bus I did a lot of thinking as I went back to the agency. I thought of things I might have told her and things I might have differently expressed. I wondered if I should tell Jewle, or wait till a more convenient moment.

Somehow I had the idea he'd be far too involved for a time with Painter and Marler to worry overmuch about Beryl.

One thing I did know was that, even if I never saw her again, I'd never forget Beryl Marport. And yet somehow I wanted to dissociate myself from that rift between her and her mother. I said that what I'd do was write an official letter to the effect that pressure of other work was making us drop the case, but that there'd be no further charge for anything we'd done.

But I didn't do it. Just before seven that evening I rang Croft House from the flat.

"This is Ludovic Travers, Lady Marport. You'll be glad to hear that at last I've located your daughter."

There was a pause. When she spoke I seemed to detect what I might call a Victorian kind of quaver.

"I'm so glad. Where is she, Mr. Travers?"

"I can't tell you. It was a condition, as it were, of my finding her. But believe me, she's well and happy. And I think she may wish to get into touch with you very soon. Real touch."

"You've given me great happiness," she said. "How can I repay you?"

"There's nothing to pay or repay," I said. "There *is* one thing you can do. I know it's presumptuous for me to advise you, but, when you do see her, try to see her point of view. She's a lovely girl, Lady Marport, and there's an enormous deal that's fine in her. You don't mind my saying that?"

"No," she said. "It was good of you."

It was as if her voice was tapering off. A second or two and she'd replaced the receiver.

You'll want to know what happened to what I might call Jewle's own case. In a way it was rather amusing, if crime can ever be that. Still, as my old French friend has said, there's always something in the misfortunes of even our friends that is not wholly displeasing to me.

The trouble began—don't quote me on this—when Marler decided to talk and his statement confirmed most of what Jewle and I had imagined. That's when a spot of trouble developed for Jewle's Higher-Ups. Jewle himself had merely obeyed instructions.

You see, the D.P.P.—I beg his pardon: The Director of Public Prosecutions—was at once in a quandary. Lady Marport had received an explicit promise that her name would be kept out of things, but Marler's confession, if Painter was charged with the murder of Dorne, made a reliance on that blackmail business an absolute necessity. The defence would see to it too. The lady in question would have had to give evidence, if only as Mrs. X, and the lady's face was far too well known. And reporters these days are most suspicious.

I understand that now there's a happy compromise. The strongest of cases has been built up against Painter for the killing of that night-watchman, and he certainly won't get off with less than twelve or fourteen years for that. If anything should happen to go wrong and a miracle happens, he could be re-arrested on discharge for the murder of Dorne. I wouldn't know. I'm no criminal lawyer: the ways of the law, in any case, are far too devious.

I still don't know just where that wretched man Marler is going to fit into things. They can't bring a charge of complicity in Dorne's murder, and for the aforementioned reasons. All they can charge him with is blackmail, and how they can do that without putting Lady Marport on the stand is something I haven't worked out. No doubt they'll find a way.

I've no tears for Dorne. That first time he'd seen me in the coffee bar, he'd known well enough who I was. The blackmail plot was already well in hand, as he'd told Painter, and on that Saturday night Painter had meant to take care that I'd do no meddling.

But somehow, I've begun to feel sorry for Marler. There was something a bit pathetic about him. He was just the weaker vessel: just a tool. If he should manage to wriggle clear I'm sure he'll slowly get back again to normality. He might even begin by shaving off that beard.

THE END